Run Sw...
in the ...
their ep...
were ba...
the turn...

Life i...
ravages...
lucky. A...
the wild... ...matters in the undergrowth; do battle with their enemy the trapper and pit their wits against the dreaded gazehounds.

A journalist and broadcaster, Tom McCaughren is a native of Ballymena, Co. Antrim. His published works include several adventure stories for children, published by the Children's Press, Dublin. He has always been interested in wildlife, an interest which promp... ...an to write *Run* ... *the Wind*, winner of the Reading Association of ... Award, 1985, and the two subsequent compan... *Run Swift, Run Free.*

D0489565

To my mother and my brother Bobby

By *Tom McCaughren*

From **WOLFHOUND PRESS**

This trilogy, *Run with the Wind, Run to Earth* and *Run Swift, Run Free* has won many awards including: The Children's Book of the Decade, 1980-1990 (Irish Children's Book Trust); White Raven Selection, 1988 (International Youth Library, Munich); Irish Book Awards Medal 1987; Reading Association of Ireland Book Award, 1985.

Run with the Wind (1983, 1984 [Twice], 1985, 1987, 1989, 1990)
  Published in Swedish by Walströms, 1987; in German by Jugund und Volk, 1988, reprinted 1989; in Japanese by Fukutake, due 1990; in UK Penguin, 1989.

Run to Earth (1984, 1986, 1987, 1989, 1990)
  Published in Swedish by Walströms, 1987; in German by Jugund und Volk, 1989; in Japanese by Fukutake, due 1990; in UK Penguin, 1989.

Run Swift, Run Free (1986, 1987, 1989, 1990)
  German and Japanese translations due 1990; in UK Penguin, 1989.

From The Children's Press
The Legend of the Golden Key (1983)
The Legend of the Phantom Highwayman (1983)
The Legend of the Corrib King (1984)
The Children of the Forge (1985)

From Anvil Books
Rainbows of the Moon (1989)

From Richview Press
The Peacemakers of Niemba, a documentary (1966)

Run *swift* Run Free

Tom McCaughren

Illustrations by Jeanette Dunne

WOLFHOUND PRESS

Reissued 1989, 1990
First paperback edition 1987
First published 1986
WOLFHOUND PRESS
68 Mountjoy Square, Dublin 1.

British Library Cataloguing in Publication Data
McCaughren, Tom
  Run swift, run free.
  I. Title
  823'.914 [J] PZ10.3

ISBN 0-86327-111-1 hardback
ISBN 0-86327-106-5 paperback

This book was first published in 1987 with the assistance of
The Arts Council/(An Chomhairle Ealaíon) Dublin, Ireland.

Cover design: Jan de Fouw
Cover Illustration: Alice Lacy
Illustrations by Jeanette Dunne
Typesetting by Design & Art Facilities (Photosetting) Ltd.
Printed and bound by Billings & Sons Ltd.

CONTENTS

'To every thing there is a season
and a time to every purpose under
the heaven . . .'

Ecclesiastes 3: 1-8.

1: A Time to be Born

THE SUN WAS SHINING from a bright blue sky, and suddenly it seemed that all the world was full of joy. Swifts sliced through the summer air with sickle-shaped wings, touched, mated in flight, and went wheeling and screaming away again.   Below them, swallows flashed across fields of lush grass that rippled and shone like an ocean in the summer breeze.   In the hedgerows, hidden by masses of hawthorn blossoms, small birds were singing as they went about their business of bringing new broods into the world.   And from somewhere farther afield and even more private, the soft lilting call of the cuckoo carried dreamily across the valley to where two fox cubs dozed in the sun.

Barely weaned, and with their faces only just lengthening into the familiar features of the fox, the cubs blissfully allowed the cuckoo's call to come in upon their consciousness.   Then their ears, which were already long and large in proportion to their young faces, turned to catch the sounds of a bumble bee as it moved among the splashes of colour which the flowers had brought to the fields.   Stirring from their slumber, they looked down at the meadows where a million buttercups shone like gold, and white stars of stitchwort sparkled in the hedgerows. Only the dandelions had gone to seed, but like many other flowers, they would bloom again; for the moment they were as nature's clock, carrying the message to the Land of Sinna that summer had come and it was time for new life to begin.

Rising, the larger cub sniffed around the bare soil outside their earth which had been flattened by their playing paws.   Then pouncing on the other cub, he caught her by surprise and bowled her over so that both rolled down the embankment into the field.   There they turned and twisted, pranced and pounced, rolled over in mock combat, parted and began a chasing game through the long grass.   Suddenly there was a yikkering sound from somewhere above them, and without pausing in their stride, they galloped up the bank and disappeared into their earth.

Almost immediately, a vixen rose from the weeds nearby.   Lifting her finely pointed nose, she sniffed the breeze, scanned the countryside for any signs of danger and followed the cubs into the earth.   As she settled in her den, the cubs climbed over her and began searching for her teats.   Snapping at them, she rose and shook them off.   Their clumsiness had hurt her.   Anyway, they were past the suckling stage and were only going for her teats through force of habit.   She settled down again and told herself that they would soon learn.   In fact, she reflected, there was a lot they must learn.

Rising again, the vixen made her way up out of the earth and from the entrance surveyed the valley once more.   For a start, she thought, they would have to learn to be on the alert for danger.   They were at that awkward in-between stage when they were neither aware of the dangers of the world nor old enough to care.

In a moment they were around her again, hanging out of her neck, pretending to bite and almost pushing her down.   She shrugged them off and as they stood back, the slow movement of her brush caught their eye.   Suddenly they were scurrying back and forth on their bellies trying to catch it – trying, but never quite succeeding.

They were thus engaged when the dog fox arrived.   The vixen was aware of his approach, but the cubs only knew of his arrival when he dropped a dead pigeon at their feet.   Immediately they pounced on it, pulling and tearing and sending a plume of downy feathers into the air.

The vixen smiled.   They were soon going to have to learn to hunt for themselves too.   It was all she and her mate could do to keep them fed.

The dog fox lay down, curled up in the sunshine and tucked his nose under the black tip of his tail.   The vixen dropped down beside him. For a while none of them spoke. Then she said, 'Black Tip.'

The dog fox opened his eyes and closed them again.

'Black Tip,' she repeated. 'We're going to have to take the cubs out soon and show them the ways of the wild.'

, Her mate grunted but didn't open his eyes.

'They've no sense,' she continued. 'No idea what's waiting for them out there. We've got to talk to them. Show them.'

'All in good time,' he replied. 'I'm worn out as it is trying to feed them.'

'That's what I mean. I'm the same. It's time we showed them how to fend for themselves.'

Black Tip was about to reply when the cubs, who had been gorging themselves, spotted another fox approaching and galloped off to meet him.

'It's Old Sage Brush,' said the vixen, and as the cubs, in their usual boisterous way began pawing and pushing and generally climbing all over the old fox, she barked and told them to stop.

Old Sage Brush eased himself down, saying, 'It's all right Vickey. They're only playing.'

Black Tip, who had got up out of respect for the old fox, lay down beside him. His mate bade the cubs to behave themselves and also settled down again.

'No need to be angry with them,' the old fox assured her. 'I may be blind but I'm not that old you know.'

Vickey knew otherwise, but she also knew he was very fond of the cubs, so she just smiled and said, 'Still, it's time they learned some manners.'

'Maybe so,' said the old fox. 'But we were all young once.'

'Sage Brush . . . ' said Vickey.

She stopped and the old fox asked her what was on her mind.

'We were thinking it was time we showed them the ways of the wild.'

Old Sage Brush knew that the prospect of cubs going out into the world was always very worrying for a vixen because of the dangers it entailed.

So did Black Tip — that was why he hadn't answered her

earlier when she had suggested it might be time.

'If they are to learn,' said the old fox, 'they must want to learn.' He paused. 'Have they reached that stage yet?'

'Not really,' Vickey admitted. 'But they're getting bigger by the day. Young Black Tip's growing by leaps and bounds, and Little Running Fox isn't far behind him.'

Realising that they were the subject of the conversation, the two cubs approached and cocked an ear. Black Tip smiled, but didn't say anything. While he shared Vickey's concern for the cubs, he took the typical dog's view that strength and high spirits were something to be admired, particularly in the dog cub which he clearly felt was the image of himself.

'I was hoping,' Vickey told the old fox, 'that you might give them the benefit of your wisdom, you know, help us to show them how to hunt and how to be cunning.'

The young dog fox sniggered at the thought of a blind fox being able to show them anything, and Vickey immediately reprimanded him for his lack of respect.

The old fox, however, just smiled, saying, 'Leave him be Vickey. He'll learn.' There was an uncomfortable silence. Then the old fox added, 'Perhaps you're right. Perhaps there is something I can show them. And maybe now's as good a time as any.' Getting to his feet, he told Young Black Tip to come with him, and walked over to the weeds.

Confidently, the young fox followed, swishing a tail which had not yet matured into a brush and which showed only a slight suggestion of the black tip which he had inherited from his father.

'Now,' said Old Sage Brush, 'tell me what you see before you Young Black Tip.'

The cub looked at the others, and then at the plant in front of him. 'A thistle,' he replied with a triumphant smile.

'That is right,' said the old fox. 'And I also can see it.'

'But how?' asked the cub.

'In my mind's eye I can see many things.'

'But that's not the same as really seeing," argued the young fox. 'I mean, you can't really see it. You can only feel it.'

'Hungry eyes see far,' the old fox told him. 'Especially when they're closed, like mine. And what advantage are yours when they are unseeing?'

'But I can see as well as any fox,' protested Young Black Tip.

'And what use is that,' asked the old fox, 'if you do not know what you are looking at?'

'I can see better than a blind fox.'

Black Tip smiled, and Vickey cast her eyes up to the skies as if to ask the great god Vulpes to forgive her son for his bad manners and his ignorance.   Little Running Fox looked at them and then at Old Sage Brush, wondering what was going on.

With the self-assurance of youth, Young Black Tip stood his ground and waited.

'If you can see better than I can,' said the old fox, 'then it should be no trouble to you to catch me.'   The young fox made to move.   'But . . .'   The old fox stopped him.   'You must not touch the thistle.'

Vickey was about to intervene as she was afraid the old fox's frail body would not be able to withstand a lunge from the cub, but Black Tip, sensing her anxiety, stopped her. 'He'll be all right,' he whispered.

Little Running Fox watched wide-eyed as her brother faced the old fox across the thistle.   She quivered with excitement and gave an involuntary hop to one side.

'Quiet,' said Old Sage Brush, then to Young Black Tip, 'Now, catch me if you can.'

The young fox immediately lowered himself on his fore-legs and dashed around the thistle.   To his surprise, he found that the old fox was now at the other side.   He tried again, with the same result.

Then he went around the other way, but the thistle was still between them.   Finally he decided that speed was the answer and thus began a dizzy chase around and around the thistle.   However it was a chase that was short-lived.   A few moments later Young Black Tip began to slow down. He staggered from the circle, his eyes rolled in his head and he collapsed.

Little Running Fox looked at her parents and seeing no signs of sympathy on their faces ran over to him.   Anxiously she nudged him with her nose, but he just groaned and rolled over on to his other side.   'What's the matter with him?' she asked.

The old fox, who also seemed a little unsteady on his feet, was coughing and trying to catch his breath.

'Nothing,' Vickey told her. 'It's just his swelled head going back down to size.'

In fact, Young Black Tip felt as if the inside of his head was spinning and that it would never stop.   When eventually it did and he was able to open his eyes, he looked up to see Old Sage Brush standing beside him.   'How is it I feel sick and you don't?' he asked him.

'Because you can see and I cannot,' replied the old fox.

Little Running Fox, who was listening intently, said, 'I don't understand.'

Her brother staggered to his feet.   'Neither do I,' he said groggily.

'It's very simple,' the old fox told him.   'You could see the world spinning around you and it made you dizzy.   I can see only what I wish to see, and even though I was running in a circle, in my mind's eye I tried to run in a straight line.'

'And you didn't get dizzy?'

'I did,' confessed the old fox, 'but not as dizzy as you.'

Young Black Tip lowered his head.   'I'm sorry Sage Brush.   I can see I've a lot to learn.'

'Well, if you can see that,' said the old fox, 'you've learned already.   Now off you go, both of you, and play – and keep an eye out for danger.'

Black Tip and Vickey smiled, and Vickey said, 'Thank you Sage Brush.'

'Sometimes you have to be cruel to be kind,' replied the old fox.

'Still, he's going to grow up to be a good strong fox,' said Black Tip.

The old fox nodded.   'Both of them will — with a little help.'

'With a little help from you maybe?' suggested Vickey.

'Maybe.'

Black Tip asked Old Sage Brush if he had visited his daughter Sinnéad who had an earth beneath the roots of a beech tree not far away.

When he nodded, Vickey remarked, 'Twinkle's getting big too.   Skulking Dog's very proud of her.'

'They both are.   She's a fine cub.'   The old fox snapped at a fly that had the temerity to land on his nose.   'How's Hop-along and She-la?'

'They're still up in the blackthorns,' Black Tip informed him.

'They're okay,' added Vickey, 'but they're having a problem with their cubs.   Two have died and one of the others is scratching himself half to death.'

The old fox got up.   'It's a pity, but man isn't our only enemy.'   He turned to go.   'If you want to send your two over to see me, you know where I am.'

'Thank you Sage Brush,' said Vickey, but the old fox was gone.

Vickey settled down again to watch the cubs, and Black Tip knew what she was thinking.   Between man and the ravages of nature, very few cubs would survive.   Perhaps one out of every litter — if they were lucky.   Sinnéad's litter had already been reduced to one, and her problem would be to ensure that she didn't lose it as well.   She-la had two left, but there was no knowing how long one of them would last.   He looked down at his own cubs. Vickey and himself were the lucky ones, he thought.   Their two were still healthy.   But what if only one of them survived?   Which one would they lose?   Would it be Little Running Fox or Young Black Tip?   It was something that didn't bear thinking about.   Yet he knew Vickey was continually thinking about it.   This was the real reason why she was irritable with the cubs.   It wasn't that she was annoyed with them; it was the frustration of knowing that their chances of becoming adult foxes were so very slim.

When the cubs had tired of romping around the field, they scampered back up to the earth, and their parents followed them inside.

While the earth was in a bank at the edge of a plantation of evergreens, the area was known to foxes far and wide as Beech Paw.   This was because of a long row of beech trees which stretched all the way from the evergreens down to the meadows.   The cubs had not been born in the earth, but in a den in a disused quarry a short distance away.   Shortly after cubbing time, Black Tip and Vickey had shared the quarry with Sinnéad and Skulking Dog, but as their cubs had grown so also had the realisation that they were too exposed to the dangers of man.   Consequently they had all moved to the safety of proper earths, Skulking Dog and Sinnéad going to the beeches, Black Tip and Vickey to the edge of the evergreens.

The move had taken place at a time when the cubs were still quite small and, not surprisingly, they had no recollection of it.   As far as they were concerned, they had always lived in the shelter of the evergreens, with the sweet scent of pine wafting in around their earth, just as it was doing now.

'I hope you've learned a lesson,' said Black Tip.

The cubs nodded.

'Sage Brush is very old and very wise,' said Vickey.

'And if it's any consolation,' Black Tip told the dog cub, 'you're not the first to make the mistake of thinking that because he has lost his sight he has lost his cunning.'

'How did he lose his sight?' asked Little Running Fox.

'One day,' said Black Tip, 'he was lying in his earth with his vixens and cubs, just like we're doing now.   Man came with his fun dogs and started probing the ground with long sticks to find out where they were.   Then they dug them out.'

'The sticks blinded the old fox,' Vickey explained, 'but he escaped with his daughter, Sinnéad.   All the others were killed.'

'Could that happen to us?' asked Little Running Fox.

Her father shook his head.   'This earth's too deep, too many tunnels.'

'But why does man hunt us?' asked Young Black Tip.   'Is it for food?'

'No,' said Vickey.   'Sometimes he brings out his small dogs and does it for fun.   Other times it's because we kill his ducks and hens.'

'That can happen at any time of the year,' said Black Tip, 'but the worst time is when the ground grows cold.   Then he puts down his choking hedge-traps and the snapping jaws.   That is when you must be very careful where you go and what you do.   That is why you must learn the lessons that we give you, and learn them well.'

Little Running Fox was puzzled.   'And he does all that

just because we take some of his birds?'

Vickey looked at her mate and then at the cubs. 'You might as well know now as later,' she told them. 'Most of the time he hunts us for our fur.'

Seeing the startled look on their faces, Black Tip added, 'But don't worry, it's no good to him when you're young or when we're in moult.'

'It's when the cold days come that you have to worry,' Vickey continued. 'Then your fur will be long and beautiful and warm. Man will want it for his own warmth and he will kill you to get it.'

'That's a long way off yet,' said Black Tip. 'But even so, he never seems to leave us alone.'

'Why does he chase us with the howling dogs?' asked Young Black Tip. 'You told us he does that in the cold days too.'

'Who knows?' said Vickey. 'Sometimes I think he doesn't need a reason.'

'And man, when he rides with the howling dogs, does he wear our fur?' asked Little Running Fox.

Her mother shook her head. 'No, his coat is a strange bright colour.'

'Like the berries you'll see on the spindle trees,' said Black Tip. 'The ones that grow over in the blackthorns.'

'And that's something you must remember,' Vickey told them. 'For when the howling dogs come, nature will hang out the spindle berries so that they shine like stars and guide you to cover.'

'Well I'm not afraid of the howling dogs,' Young Black Tip asserted. 'I'll outrun them.'

'Hopefully you will,' said Vickey. 'But Old Sage Brush has taught us that strength is not enough. When the howling dogs come they can also bring a great sense of fear, a fear that can make you do stupid things.'

Black Tip nodded. 'The fear of the fear, the old fox calls it. You must be strong enough to overcome that first. Then you may have a chance. But you will need much cunning to go with your strength — all the cunning that the great god Vulpes has given you.'

'Where did you learn all these things?' asked Little Running Fox.

'We learned from our parents,' Vickey told her. 'Just as you are learning from us. But we also learned much from Old Sage Brush.' The cubs snuggled closer, and she went on, 'You see, before you were born, there were very few of us left and we were afraid we'd all be wiped out.'

'Man had become more cunning than ourselves,' said Black Tip. 'But Old Sage Brush has lived a long time, and he is very wise.'

'So one night,' Vickey recalled, 'we met him down under the beech trees. We asked him to show us how he, a blind fox, could survive when others couldn't.'

'And did he?' asked Young Black Tip.

'Yes. Some, like you, laughed at the thought of getting a blind fox to show them anything. But it was their loss. We went on a long journey with him. We faced many dangers, but we learned much.'

'Who went with you?' asked Little Running Fox.

'Skulking Dog,' said Black Tip. 'That's where he met Sinnéad. He rescued her from the howling dogs you know.'

'Did he?' asked the dog cub in admiration. 'I didn't know that.'

'There's a lot you don't know,' said Vickey. 'Hop-along went with us in spite of the fact that he has only three legs. That took not only strength but great courage.'

'Scat never told me that. Nor Scab.'

'That's because they don't know,' his father told him. 'Hop-along isn't one to talk of his courage, especially to his own cubs.'

'Did She-la go?' asked Little Running Fox.

Vickey nodded. 'She's a very brave fox too. When we returned, man was building a dam across the lake to make it bigger and he caught her unawares down in the meadows. She was shot and her cubs were born when she was in a deep sleep. But she fought back and got better. Now she does most of the hunting for her family.'

'When are we going to learn to hunt?' asked Young Black Tip.

'Soon,' said his father.

'And when will that be?' asked Little Running Fox.

Vickey smiled. 'Sooner than you think.'

2: A Time to Plant

BLUEBELLS WHICH EARLIER had made a quiet, almost shy appearance in the hedgerows, now formed a carpet of colour beneath the trees at Beech Paw, while out in the fields, large daisies which had eased their way up through the long grass, nodded in the breeze and glanced with golden eyes at the sun.

It's doubtful, however, if the cubs even noticed these subtle changes in their surroundings as they made their way through the fields. All they were interested in was food. The only things they had hunted so far were black beetles, slugs and worms, and that had been in the vicinity of their earth. Now they were going out into the world and they were on the lookout for something bigger.

Having hunted in turns during the night so as not to tire themselves out, Black Tip and Vickey had made sure the cubs had received just the right amount of food. They didn't want them to be so full they wouldn't have the will to hunt, or so hungry that they might do something rash that would put their lives in danger.

Even so, they found it wasn't easy to keep the cubs in check. They would dash off towards the slightest movement or sound, and of course, their clumsiness always ensured that there was nothing there when they arrived. The same happened when they spotted a rabbit nibbling grass not far from its burrow. They charged headlong at it, only to see its short white tail flashing into a burrow before they were even half way there.

Black Tip smiled. 'Rabbits may be stupid,' he told them,

'but they're not slow.   Now, while you're here, examine the ground and remember what you see.'

As the cubs began to nose around, Vickey pointed to a small root just inside the entrance of the burrow, saying, 'Here, look at this.'

The cubs peered at the root.

'Well, what do you notice about it?'

'There are small hairs on the end of it,' observed Little Running Fox.

'That's right, and if there are no rabbits to be seen, that's the sort of thing that will tell you a burrow is occupied. Now what else do you see?'

The cubs examined the entrance more closely.   'Nothing,' said Young Black Tip at last.

'And what does that tell you?'

The dog cub looked at his mother, puzzled.   'If there's nothing there how can it tell us anything?'

Black Tip, who had been listening, came closer and told them, 'The very fact that there's nothing more to be seen is another way of knowing it's occupied.'

'You see,' Vickey explained, 'it's because rabbits are using it that there are no cobwebs across the entrance, no grass growing on the way in.   These are things you must learn to look for.'

'And don't forget the droppings,' added Black Tip.   'Look, over there.   Those are rabbit droppings.'

The cubs examined the droppings with great curiosity.

'They're like dew-drops,' observed Little Running Fox.

'Not a bit like ours,' said her brother.

'That's because all animals are different,' their father told them.   'They all leave different tracks, different scents and different droppings.   These are round, like the berries you will see on the bushes.   You can't mistake them.   Now off you go and see if you can find any more.'

'And be careful,' warned Vickey as they raced away.

'They haven't a clue,' Black Tip remarked.

'I know,' said Vickey, 'but they'll learn.'

A short time later the cubs came charging back in a high state of excitement to say they had found signs of rabbits in another field.

'Good,' replied Black Tip.   'Lead on.'

Coming to a field where the grass was short and sparse, the cubs led their parents to a pile of droppings. Vickey tittered and Black Tip tried to suppress a smile.

'What are you laughing at?' asked Young Black Tip. 'That's what you told us to look out for.'

Vickey was still smiling. 'You're both looking with your eyes, but not your nose.'

'These droppings are too big and too black to belong to a rabbit,' Black Tip told them. 'Anyway, your nose should tell you they belong to sheep, not to rabbits!'

'You mean they're sheep's droppings?' asked Little Running Fox.

'Of course they are,' replied her mother. 'Can't you see, they're all over the field.'

Disappointed, the cubs lay down and began to sulk.

'There's no need to feel that way about it,' said Black Tip. 'We all make mistakes.'

'And you must learn from them,' said Vickey. She paused before adding, 'It's what Old Sage Brush was saying when he played the game around the thistle. Your eyes will tell you some things, but not all. You must use your other senses too . . . your sense of smell, your hearing, but above all, your cunning.'

'And how do we do that?' asked Young Black Tip.

'You must listen to us,' said his father, 'and to foxes like Old Sage Brush. How do you think he has lived so long? How do you think he catches his food? Only great cunning and wisdom can make up for the loss of sight.'

'Even Ratwiddle has a strange sort of wisdom,' Vickey told them.

Having met Ratwiddle once when he stopped by their earth, Young Black Tip had an impulse to laugh. Then he remembered what had happened when he had laughed at Old Sage Brush, so he just said, 'But he's very odd, isn't he? I mean, he spends all his time down at the river catching rats.'

'Maybe so,' Vickey continued, 'but the only fox you may laugh at is yourself. Do not sulk at your mistakes; laugh at them and learn.'

The cub smiled, and she added, 'Come now and I'll show you how to catch a rabbit.'

Leading them towards a hedgerow where she knew there was a rabbit warren, Vickey circled around until they were facing into the breeze.   'Now,' she told them, 'you must always remember that our scent can be carried in the wind. For that reason you must always hunt into the wind and run with it.'

'When you're hunting rabbits,' said Black Tip, 'you'll find that they are always on the alert for danger.   Their ears are long and their eyes are large.   Not only that, but their eyes are in the sides of their heads so they can see anything that's creeping up on them.'

'How do you catch them then?' asked Young Black Tip.

'By being smarter than they are,' said Vickey.   'Now keep quiet and watch.'

Edging forward, they peered through a hawthorn hedge into the next field.   On the left of the field, beneath an older hedge, was a bank riddled with burrows.   A short distance out from it, a number of rabbits were feeding.   They nibbled and hopped, looked up and listened, and all the time stayed within safe distance of their burrows.

Slipping through the hawthorns, Vickey trotted across the field.   Immediately the rabbits bolted into their holes. However she ignored them, continued on past and disappeared through the hedge at the far end.

'What's she doing?' asked Young Black Tip.

'Just keep quiet and you'll see,' said his father.

When the rabbits were satisfied the fox had gone, they ventured out again, and after a while Vickey trotted back across the field.   This time, it appeared to the cubs, she was a little nearer to the warren than she had been the first time. The rabbits again ran for cover, but because she continued to ignore them, they weren't so long in coming back out.

'That's the whole idea,' whispered Vickey when she rejoined the cubs, and before they could ask her what she meant, she slipped over into the field for a third time and trotted past the warren once more.   This time some of the rabbits only ran as far as the entrance to their burrows, and as soon as she had gone continued to feed out in the field.

The cubs watched and waited, and when Vickey re-appeared they saw that several of the rabbits didn't even bother to run.   Instead they just sat and stared as she lay down opposite them and began to scratch herself.

If the cubs were curious to know what their mother was doing, the rabbits were equally curious, and some more of them ventured to the entrance to their burrows to find out what was going on.

Acting as if they didn't exist, Vickey rolled over and over in the grass. Then, getting to her feet, she did another peculiar thing. She began to chase her tail. As she spun round and round, the rabbits continued to stare at her, mesmerised by her strange behaviour.

To the cubs, who were no less intrigued by what she was doing, it seemed as if she was playing the game with the thistle. This, however, was a different game, and it didn't last long, as both they and the rabbits discovered a moment later.

Breaking out of her circle, Vickey suddenly sped towards the nearest rabbit. Taken by surprise, it was unable to get past the other rabbits which had gathered around the entrance to the burrows. She was upon it in an instant and when she returned to the cubs she dropped it at their feet.

'That's a lot of trouble to go to for one rabbit,' Young Black Tip remarked.

They were trotting up along a hedgerow towards the line of blackthorns that stretched across the brow of the hill.

'There's no easy way to hunt,' his mother told him. 'You have to work hard for everything you get.'

'Unless it's some old crow that's already dead,' said his father, 'and you won't get fat on the likes of that.'

Little Running Fox said nothing. She was carrying the rabbit and was obviously very proud of herself.

Hop-along was sitting in the sun outside his earth when they arrived, and She-la, his mate, came out when she heard them talking.

'We thought maybe you could use some extra food,' said Black Tip.

'To help train the cubs,' added Vickey, anxious not to offend them,. 'We think it's time ours started hunting for themselves.'

Before either of them could reply, Scat sped up out of the earth and pounced on the rabbit. Not to be outdone, Young Black Tip and Little Running Fox immediately joined in.   A bark from She-la stopped them, and taking the rabbit she buried it nearby.   'It'll do for later,' she said.   'Thanks.'

'Who caught it?' asked Hop-along.   'Running Fox?'

Black Tip shook his head.   'It was Vickey.   We're just showing them how.'

'They'll need all the help they can get,' said Hop-along.

'How's Scab?' asked Vickey.

'Still the same,' She-la told her.   She gave a bark and her other cub came up out of the earth.

Scab was a pitiful sight.   He suffered from an itch which had made him scratch himself until he was sore.   Even when bits of his fur had fallen out he had continued to scratch until he was raw.   Scabs had formed, but even his tail looked as if it had been attacked by moths.

'How are you?' asked Black Tip.

'All right,' Scab told him.   'If only the itch would go away.'

'Have you tried soaking him in the river?' Vickey asked his mother.

She-la nodded.   'But it's no good.'

Scab went back into the earth.

'If it was fleas,' She-la went on, 'the water would get rid of them.   But it must be something else.   I just hope I don't lose him too.'

'How come none of the rest of you have it?' Black Tip asked her.

'After the other two died from it, we gave him a place where he could sleep on his own.   We didn't want him giving it to Scat.   It's hard on him, but he just has to keep to himself.'

'And Scat's all right?' asked Vickey.

'Look at him,' said She-la.   'He's small, but he's as hardy as a stoat.'

'How are you going to teach them to hunt?' inquired Black Tip.   'I mean, between hunting yourselves and trying to get Scab better, you're going to have your work cut out.'

'We'll manage,' said Hop-along.   'I've already told them a thing or two.'

'We were thinking we might send our two over to see Old Sage Brush,' Vickey told them.   'If we do, do you want to send yours along too?'

'Do you think the old fox would mind?' asked She-la.

Vickey shook her head. 'I don't think so. He was wondering how you all were.'

'Well, we'll see how it goes,' said Hop-along.   'If it's not a fox with only three legs, it's one that's blind.   That's the way man has left us.'

'Would you listen to him,' scoffed Black Tip.   'The only fox I know that has put his leg in the snapping jaws and lived to tell the tale.'

'Anyway,' said Vickey, 'if you want to send them over to Old Sage Brush, let us know.   We're going down to the river to show ours how to fish.   Do you want to come along?'

Hop-along shook his head and She-la said, 'We'll stay here and keep an eye on Scab.   I don't think he's in form for going.   But you can take Scat if you like.'

Scat was off with the other two cubs before another word could be said, and Black Tip and Vickey trotted after them.

As they made their way across the side of the valley, the sun sparkled on the lake below and reflected the Mountain of Vulpes rising on the far side.

'Hop-along's a bit down in the mouth,' Vickey remarked.

'He often gets like that,' said Black Tip.   'It must be hard on him, having only three legs.'

'And I don't like the look of Scab.   They must be very worried about him.'

Black Tip agreed.   'We must talk to Old Sage Brush again and ask him what he thinks.'

Scat, on the other hand, was everything his mother said he was.   He was full of energy and was determined not to be outdone by any other cub, whether in running, fighting — albeit in fun — or in hunting.   Thus when a rabbit burst into life and scudded into a patch of gorse, he was on to it first.   The other two cubs raced after him and were close on his heels when they were pulled up short by a sharp bark from Vickey.   Scat continued, but remembering what they had been told about the futility of such a chase, Young Black Tip and Little Running Fox waited expectantly to see what their mother was going to do.

To their surprise, Vickey told them to stay with their father, and bounded after Scat.   Entering the gorse with considerably more caution than he had done, she found him at the rabbit burrow, and with an angry snap at his hind-quarters, chased him back out.

'What did you do that for?' he asked indignantly, when they had rejoined the others.   'I was only chasing a rabbit.'

'I know you were,' said Vickey sternly.   'But you must never run into thick cover like that again.   Never.   And that goes for all of you.   If you don't put your head in a choking hedge-trap, you're liable to put your paw into the snapping jaws.'

'The trapper is just waiting for you to make a mistake like that,' explained Black Tip.   'He knows that a fox may dash into gorse after a rabbit, or may lie under it and wait for one.'

'So he places his trap under the gorse,' added Vickey.

'But there wasn't one,' said Scat, 'so I'm all right.'

'You're all right this time,' said Vickey, 'but you're lucky.'

'You mean there *is* a trap in there?' asked Little Running Fox.

Vickey nodded, and Scat said, 'I didn't see any.'

'That's because you didn't take the time to look,' Vickey told him.   'Now follow me and I'll show you.   But be careful and stick to the path behind me.'

The cubs watched as she crept into the gorse and then eased herself down on her belly.   'It's in there,' she said, 'just off the path.'

The cubs could now see a rusty steel trap lying on its side.

'But the snapping jaws are closed,' Scat observed.

'They're closed now,' Vickey replied, 'but they were open when they were put there.   Something must have disturbed them.'

'That's the type of trap Hop-along caught his leg in,' Black Tip informed them.

'But how did he get out of it?' asked Scat.

'He chewed his leg off,' said Vickey.

Horrified at the thought, the cubs pulled back.

'How could he do such a thing?' asked Little Running Fox.

'He had no option,' Black Tip told her.   'It was either that, or die.'

'Now come closer,' said Vickey, 'and I'll show you how to deal with a trap like this.'

Getting to her feet, she lifted the trap in her mouth and dropped it on to the path. The others could see that it was still attached to the bottom of a gorse bush by a chain, and they watched as she nosed dried grass and gorse needles on to it until it was covered.

'The trapper always covers it like that,' she explained, 'so you have to look for it, and this is the way to do it.' Going down on her belly again, she crawled forward until her paws came in contact with the trap. 'The jaws will be open,' she said, 'but you will be all right so long as you don't put your paw into the middle of it.' Shuffling forward again, she edged the trap ahead of her and sideways until she had it in off the path. 'Now,' she added, 'that's how you deal with the snapping jaws and clear the way to go in after your rabbit.'

Black Tip backed out into the field, and taking great care not to put a paw wrong, the cubs did likewise.

'I could have ended up just like my father,' said Scat, 'with just three legs.'

Vickey gave him another stern look, and told him, 'You could have ended up dead. It takes a lot of courage to chew your leg off. Remember that.'

'Anyway,' said Black Tip, 'you know what to look out for now and how to deal with it. I've seen Hop-along spring the snapping jaws shut by dropping a stick on them, but you have to be careful they don't jump up and catch you. I'm sure he'll show you himself.'

Scat wasn't in such a hurry to race ahead after that. Nor indeed were the other two. It was beginning to dawn on them that there was more to this hunting business than they had thought.

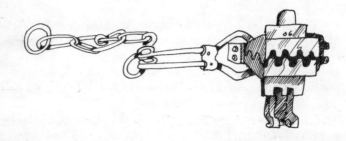

When they were just above the dam which man had built across the floor of the valley to make the lake larger, they lay down among the rushes and buttercups to take stock. Sheep and cows grazed in the fields below them, and farther down meadow pipits fluttered in the breeze.

Here and there at the edge of the lake, mallard ducks and coots turned their tails to the sky as they up-ended themselves in search of food beneath the surface.   The birds in turn held out the prospect of food for the foxes, but they could see that man was present on the dam, so they decided against going down to the lake.   The river offered more cover, for below the dam it continued the way it always had done, tumbling down through the rocks, disappearing in places between alder trees and willows, and shining like a silvery eel as it meandered through the meadows beyond.

On the next hill, they could see a small plantation of evergreens and they decided to head for that.   From there they could view the river and discuss their next move.   They reached it a short time later and were just settling down beneath the outer branches when Little Running Fox exclaimed, 'There's Ratwiddle.'   The others got up and focussed their eyes on the river bank.   'There, at the alder trees,' she told them.

'What's he doing?' asked Young Black Tip.

'What he's always doing,' said his father.   'Hunting for rats.'

'That's a funny name for a fox,' Scat remarked.

Young Black Tip smiled.   'He's a funny fox.'

'The way he goes around with his head in the air you'd think he doesn't want to talk to anybody,' said Little Running Fox.   'But he's all right really.'

'But how did he ever get a name like Ratwiddle?' asked Scat.

'We used to think it was from catching water rats,' Vickey told him.   'You know, that the rat's widdle had given him a sickness.'

'And made his neck stiff,' said Little Running Fox.

'The rats had something to do with it all right,' continued Vickey, 'but not the way we thought.'

'As far as we can make out he was caught in a choking hedge-trap once,' said Black Tip.   'The rats attacked him, and it sort of turned his mind a bit.'

'But don't go thinking it has made him stupid,' warned Vickey. 'He can be wise in his own peculiar way. It's just that it's difficult to know what he means sometimes.'

'Can we go down to him?' asked Young Black Tip.

'Maybe he can show us how to fish,' suggested Little Running Fox. 'Please, can we?'

'All right,' said Vickey, 'but be careful. And don't be teasing him. We'll follow you down in a little while.'

Excited at the prospect of going down to the river on their own and meeting Ratwiddle, the three cubs raced away through the grass.

In a gap between the alder trees, the bank gave way to a patch of shingle that jutted out into the shallows, and there Ratwiddle sat scratching himself. It was well known that he had fleas and even the cubs knew it wasn't healthy to go too close to him. As usual his head was cocked at an angle in the air, almost as if he didn't want to see them.

Young Black Tip smiled and said, 'Hallo Ratwiddle, have you caught anything yet?'

The other two giggled, but Ratwiddle ignored them and continued to scratch.

'I mean, have you caught any rats?' added Young Black Tip.

When he still didn't answer, Little Running Fox asked him, 'Why do you keep watching the sky?'

Ratwiddle stopped scratching, and lowering his head stiffly, told her, 'If you don't look up you won't see the water.'

Thinking he was making some kind of joke, the cubs laughed. However he didn't seem to think it was funny, and ignoring them again, he trotted off.

'He's daft,' said Scat.

Young Black Tip agreed. 'His head's in the clouds. I don't know how he ever catches anything — rats or fleas!'

Little Running Fox had already forgotten him and was nosing around at the edge of the water. 'Look,' she said, 'fish.'

The other two bounded over, and she showed them a small shoal of minnows darting through the shallows. They all edged closer and their eyes opened wide as they

focussed on the cluster of shadowy shapes that twisted and turned just below the surface.   For a moment they watched, their heads moving from side to side with every change of direction that the minnows took.   Then, with one accord, they all crashed in, chopping at the water and trying to pin the elusive fish to the bottom with their paws.

Under the evergreens, Black Tip and Vickey looked at each other and cast their eyes up to the sky.   At the same time they couldn't help smiling, for they knew that while the cubs weren't going to catch anything, they were having a lot of fun.

Black Tip lowered his head, tucked his nose under the tip of his tail and dozed.   Vickey, however, remained vigilant, ever watchful for any sign of danger.   In the distance, to her right, she could see the dam and the white streaks on it reminded her of a badger's head.   She got up.   A sense of unease had begun to spread through her body.

Black Tip half opened his eyes. 'What's wrong?' he mumbled.

Vickey looked down at the cubs.   'I don't know, maybe nothing.   It's just a feeling I have.'   The cubs were still frolicking about in the river.   She looked back at the dam and suddenly it dawned on her what was wrong.   It was the white streaks.   It hadn't occurred to her the first time what they were.   But now she knew.   They were torrents of water spewing from the dam as man released it from the lake!

Vickey glanced at the river again, and to her dismay saw that she was right.   A wall of water was already rolling down the river towards the cubs.   For a moment she was seized with panic.   'Black Tip!' she cried.

Jumping to his feet, Black Tip also saw the water bearing down on the cubs.   Vickey screamed at them, but they were too far away, and in a desperate effort to warn them, flung herself down the hillside.

Black Tip arrived at the river barely a fox-length behind her, only to find that they were too late.   The cubs had gone and in their place was a mass of brown muddy water which had already spilled over into the fields.

3: A Time to Pluck Up

THE WALL OF WATER had borne down on the three cubs without warning. There was no roaring noise, no rushing sound; instead it had crept upon them as silently as the wind and with the stealth of a hunter. When they looked up, it was too late. Suddenly they were enveloped in dark swirling currents which swept them off their feet, choking them, blinding them, turning them head over heels and banging them against a never-ending succession of unseen objects which were being carried along beside them. It was as if they had fallen into a thicket of thorns, or a clump of nettles, which pricked and stung and tormented them at every twist and turn, until unconsciousness finally poured in upon them bringing a calm that usually can be found only in sleep.

A short time later, like an owl unable to digest the bones of a mouse, the swollen river disgorged Little Running Fox and Scat, and left them lying in a pool of floodwater. In their subconscious they were still aware of the river, and awoke to what they thought was the water lapping up around their faces. Through watery eyes they saw it was Black Tip and Vickey licking them back to life, and as they came around they began to cough and splutter and heave in an effort to expel the water from their lungs.

Black Tip and Vickey helped them to their feet and led them to the safety of higher ground. Then as Vickey tended to their bruised bodies, Black Tip sped off in search of the other cub. Anxiously Vickey watched him go and prayed to the great god Vulpes that he would find him.

Young Black Tip had been swept far down-river, and it was only as the flood began to spread and lose its power that it loosened its grip and let him go. He awoke to the gentle ebb and flow of a river recovering from a mighty disturbance, and found that the flood had deposited him across the lower branches of an alder tree. It was a moment or two before he realised what was holding his head above the water, and as his body convulsed and gasped for air, he was grateful that the alder had reached out to take him.

When he had recovered, he struggled across the submerged branches and pulled himself up on to a log that was half in and half out of the river. There he lay and watched weeds, twigs and other flotsam swirling around in the muddy water. He coughed again and was getting up to go when something else caught his eye. A dead rat, he thought, and edging down to the water reached out and pulled it on to the log. He smiled to himself. It might not be the fish they had been hoping to catch, but at least it was something to show for all their trouble.

Getting to his feet, he shook himself and was about to lift the sodden body when he saw by the movement of its belly that it was still breathing. At the same time the creature opened its beady little eyes, twitched its blunt snout and sneezed. Startled, he drew back, saying, 'I thought you were dead.'

The little creature struggled shakily to its feet. 'So did I.' It shook itself, sending a shower of water into his face. 'I mean, I felt sure I was going to be drowned. What happened? Did you pull me out?'

Young Black Tip nodded. 'I thought rats were good swimmers.'

'I'm not a rat. I'm a mink.'

'But you're small, and you look like a drowned rat. Anyway, I thought mink were good swimmers.'

'So we are, but I'm only learning.'

The little mink staggered and lay down again. Seeing that it was so exhausted it could hardly stand, Young Black Tip said, 'Here, let me help you.'

Young and all as the mink was, it was suspicious and asked, 'Are you going to kill me?'

Young Black Tip shook his head. The thought had

occurred to him, but he felt sorry for it. 'You're just learning, like me,' he said.   'Come on.   I'll take you on to the bank.'

Picking it up in his mouth, he turned and made his way up along the log.   But even as he hopped on to the grass which had been flattened by the floodwater, he saw a blurr out of the corner of his eye, and before he could turn his head he was bowled over.   The little mink was knocked from his mouth and was sent rolling across the grass.

Picking himself up, Young Black Tip looked around to see what had happened and found he was face to face with a full-grown she-mink.   From the protective manner in which she was standing over the young one, he knew immediately she was its mother.   She was almost like an otter, he thought, only much smaller, and her body was slender and sinuous, like a stoat.   Her neck was thick and strong, and her small head held no fear of him as she stared, lips twitching, teeth bared in a show of aggression.

He stepped forward to explain that he hadn't meant the little mink any harm.   Immediately she rushed at him,

forcing him to step back so fast that he almost tripped and fell.

The young mink was beginning to recover now, and seeing what was happening, told its mother, 'He was only trying to help me.'

The she-mink went back and standing over it again, said, 'I told you never to trust foxes. They're up to all sorts of tricks.'

'But he pulled me out of the flood. If it wasn't for him I'd have drowned.'

'Pulled you out to eat you more likely.'

'He could have, but he didn't. He said I was just learning like himself.'

The she-mink lowered her head, and Young Black Tip could see she was becoming less aggressive.

'Well,' she told the little mink, 'at least you're safe. But foxes are hunters like ourselves. Keep away from them.'

Young Black Tip was now aware of his father by his side, and saw the aggressive look returning to the face of the mother mink. Without taking her eyes off them, she retreated a few steps, picked up the young one and bounded off through the undergrowth.

Whatever fears the mink might have had, Vickey was afraid she would never see her dog cub again, and when her mate returned with him, she was overjoyed. However, it was a joy that was short-lived.

As they returned to Beech Paw she began to blame herself for letting them go down to the river on their own. She had forgotten that man occasionally let water out of the dam, and she should have remembered. Then her concern for them turned to annoyance.

'I told you you should listen to Ratwiddle,' she said. 'He has a strange way of saying things, but he's wise enough. When he said he was looking at the sky to see the water, you should have tried to figure out what he meant.'

Black Tip agreed. 'He has a funny way of putting things all right, but that was his way of telling you he was keeping an eye on the dam.'

Vickey threw an angry look at her dog cub. 'And making friends with a mink! We didn't bring you out to make friends; we brought you out to show you how to hunt.'

Young Black Tip lowered his head, and his father told him, 'The she-mink was right, you know.   You should have been up to your tricks.'   They trotted on in silence.   'But then,' he added, 'maybe she would have killed you.   Mink can be fierce fighters, especially when their young are in danger.'

Vickey nodded.   'Well, maybe it all worked out for the best.   But I think it's time Old Sage Brush had a word with them.   Perhaps he can put some sense into them.'

The cubs kept their heads down and said nothing.   They reckoned it was one of those times when Vickey would say what she felt she had to say and wasn't interested in any views but her own.   Consequently they continued in silence until they arrived back at Scat's earth.

When Hop-along and She-la heard what had happened, they told Scat to get below and not to come out until they said he could.

'I suppose it's not his fault really,' said She-la.   'To tell the truth, we haven't been able to give him much training, what with Scab the way he is.'

'And me the way I am,' admitted Hop-along.   'It's all I can do to hunt for myself.'

'How about sending them over to see the old fox then?' suggested Vickey.   'They could go with our two.'

'Is Sinnéad sending Twinkle?' asked She-la.

'We haven't talked to her yet,' said Vickey.   'but if she is, we'll let you know and maybe they can all go together.'

'Do you think they'd be safe?'

'We'd keep an eye on them,' Black Tip assured her.   'Don't worry, they'd be all right.'

'Well, if Twinkle was going, I suppose two more wouldn't make much difference,' said Hop-along.   'Let us know.'

Black Tip and Vickey were fully aware of the reasons why Hop-along and She-la were reluctant to send their cubs to Old Sage Brush.   Both of them knew the old fox was frail and they didn't want to impose upon him.   But it was also a question of pride.   They were slow to admit, even to themselves, that they couldn't cope with their own problems, especially Hop-along's handicap.   If, on the other hand, Sinnéad and her mate, Skulking Dog, were also looking to the old fox for help, then that would change the situation; they too could accept his assistance without loss of face.

However, when Black Tip and Vickey called to see Sinnéad in her earth beneath the beech trees, they found that Skulking Dog had taken Twinkle out and was showing her how to hunt himself.

'You know what he's like', smiled Sinnéad. 'He's so independent. He won't accept advice from anyone, not even Old Sage Brush and he's my own father.'

'Where has he gone?' asked Black Tip.

'Up over the hill. He said he wouldn't be back until after dark.'

Neither Black Tip nor Vickey said anything, but they were both thinking the same thing. Even on the journey they had taken with Old Sage Brush, Skulking Dog had not been able to resist the temptation to raid a hen-house, and it had nearly got him killed. If that's what he was planning on doing now, he'd have to be doubly careful as the trapper lived on the other side of the hill.

The trapper lived alone in a small bungalow in a wood of beech trees, ash and occasional oak. It was said that he could snare a pheasant with a horse hair, and catch goldfinches with a pyramid of hazels using a circle of spindlewood as a spring. A thin, wiry man who chewed tobacco when he wasn't smoking his pipe, he spent many of his summer evenings making snares from pieces of cable and wire which he salvaged from a nearby rubbish dump. His hands were grubby and his nails broken and bruised, but they were hands that were hardened and able to twist a noose that would hold the most determined fox.

He had lived over in Glensinna until it had been turned into a reservoir, and he knew that those who had been able to remain in the valley were glad to see him go. *Gleann an tSionnaigh Bháin* they called it. The Valley of the White Fox. He smiled to himself. What a superstitious lot. They believed that so long as foxes continued to live in the valley, so would they. There were even those who had given the fox credit for the fact that when the dam was built, the water hadn't risen far enough to cover their

homes. However, superstition was a luxury he couldn't afford. The fox hadn't saved his home, but now he had a new one. He also had several new dogs, and his fox furs had helped to pay for them.

Taking up a pliers, he twisted a nail into the shape of a swivel that would allow a fox to twist and turn without breaking the snare. 'That'll hold him m'boy,' he grunted. A small black mongrel which was lying at his feet enjoying the heat of the stove, pricked up its ears and looked at him. He worked away at the wire, observing that it was good and strong, and when he had finished he hung it with a bundle of others on a peg behind the door.

Returning to his chair, he took out his pipe, dipped it into a plastic pouch and fingered tobacco into the bowl. The dog went over to the door, put its nose to the bottom and whimpered. Outside, his other dogs, a German pointer and two greyhounds, began to bark, and there was an uncomfortable cackle from the hen-house. 'It's all right boy,' he said to the mongrel. 'I know they're out there.'

The little dog came back and lay down at his feet, but it

was uneasy.   Every now and then it lifted its head, which was deeply scarred from many an underground battle, and twitched its ears.

The trapper struck a match on the stove, sucked on his pipe, and expelled lungfuls of blue smoke.   Then he threw the spent match in the direction of the grate and leaned back in his chair.   'All in good time,' he said to the dog.   'All in good time.'   He had seen the cubs over at the long row of beeches, and he knew that when they were mature they would bring him a good price, especially if they were snared and the pelts were undamaged.   He fingered the fox paw that hung around his neck.   'Lucky as a rabbit's foot,' he told the dog.

Outside, the other dogs were restless again.   The trapper smiled and got ready for bed.   He wouldn't harm the foxes, for the time being at any rate, provided they didn't harm him.

When the days were warm, Skulking Dog told his cub, they were always too long.   The nights were the best time to hunt, but they were too short.

'Man can't see in the dark,' he explained, 'so he goes to sleep.'

'His fun dogs are awake,' whispered Twinkle.

'But they're not free.   Listen, you can tell from their bark.'

They were lying beneath the trees at the edge of the wood.   Before them the bungalow and several out-houses were clearly visible in the light of the moon.

'Vulpes is good,' said Skulking Dog.   'He has sent the wide eye of gloomglow to help us.'

Twinkle looked up at the moon, and then scanned the sky for the little pinpoints of light from which she had got her name.   Her mother had told her she had such a spot on her forehead and that it was very beautiful, but she had never seen it herself.   The moon, she could see, was round and bright, almost like their own eyes, and she could understand why her parents called it the wide eye of gloomglow.

'Come on,' whispered Skulking Dog.   'This is no time to be looking around you.   Keep your eyes skinned in case he lets any of his fun dogs loose.   If he does I'll try and draw them off.'

Twinkle kept close to her father. She knew he was a fearless hunter, and she was anxious to learn as much as possible from him. The thought of being so near to the fun dogs frightened her, but she said nothing to betray her fears. They passed an old rabbit hutch in which the trapper kept his ferrets and she found the smell most offensive. Then they were at the wire pens where the dogs were kept.

All the dogs were standing on their hind legs, pawing at the wire and barking loudly. One dog, she could see, had big jaws, strong legs and a stumpy tail. The other two were even more odd-looking. They were taller and thinner, so thin she could see their ribs in the light of gloomglow. Even their legs and tails were thin. Their noses were long and pointed and their mouths were full of the most savage teeth she had ever seen.

From the direction of the house another, smaller dog, began to bark. Skulking Dog looked back and seeing that everywhere was in darkness, hurried on towards the hen-shed. Both the sound and the smell of the dogs sent a shiver down Twinkle's back, and she kept so close to her father that in the shadows their shapes almost merged into one.

Although the hens were closed in for the night, they could also sense the presence of intruders. Man might say that their powers of smell and hearing are very limited, but animals and birds have their own way of knowing when they are in danger, and the hens had become very restless on their roosts.

Skulking Dog glanced back at the house again. It was still in darkness, so he quietly nosed around the hen-shed to see if there was any way he could get in.

Twinkle found the smell coming from the hen-shed very tempting, but then as she began to sniff around, she got a whiff of something else, something outside the shed. She immediately followed it up, and nearby discovered a hen's foot sticking out of the ground. Grabbing it, she pulled and pulled until, to her delight, she unearthed the carcase of a chicken.

Seeing what she had found, Skulking Dog whispered, 'Well done. It may not be good enough for man, but it will do us nicely.   And we didn't even have to break in to get it.'

Twinkle didn't reply — her mouth was full — but there was no need.   As she trotted back through the wood, her prize grasped tightly in her jaws, Skulking Dog could see she was very proud of herself.   He also felt proud; their first night out hunting together and his daughter was bringing something home.   It was always a great moment for a hunter.

Sinnéad, who had been waiting anxiously at the entrance to their earth, was greatly relieved when Twinkle returned safely, and she shared her mate's feeling of pride when she heard what had happened.   However, as Twinkle lay down and hungrily munched the chicken, she began to feel unwell.

'What's the matter?' asked Sinnéad.

'Pains,' gasped Twinkle.   'In my stomach.'

Skulking Dog rushed over to them.   'Is it very bad?' Twinkle nodded and he told her, 'Don't eat any more.   Just lie still.'

Sinnéad looked at him, startled.   'You don't think the trapper could have left it out deliberately, do you?'

Skulking Dog was silent.   Suddenly it all made sense . . . no lights in the house, the fun dogs in their pens, a chicken buried just outside the hen-shed.   He took a deep breath and nodded.   'He must have put something in it.'

'Poison!' exclaimed Sinnéad.   'What are we going to do?' She looked at Twinkle who was now groaning with pain. 'Quick,' she told Skulking Dog. 'Get Vickey.   Maybe she'll know.'

As her mate sped off through the beech trees towards the evergreens, Sinnéad lay down beside Twinkle and tried to comfort her.   'Hold on,' she whispered.   'Hold on, and whatever you do, don't go to sleep.'

Black Tip and Vickey arrived a few moments later.

'What are we going to do?' asked Sinnéad.

Vickey was looking at Twinkle closely.   'Has she eaten much of it?'

Sinnéad nodded. 'A good bit.'

'Old Sage Brush,' said Vickey.   'He'll know what to do — if we can get him in time.'

Black Tip and Skulking Dog were already on their way,

and as they disappeared into the darkness, Vickey cried after them, 'Hurry. We'll try and keep her awake until you come back. Hurry.'

Twinkle's eyes were closed, her mouth was dry, and she was feeling cold. Sinnéad and Vickey lay on each side of her to keep her warm and talked to her. They told her how she had done very well to find the chicken, and how strong she had been to carry it home on her own.

'Just imagine,' said Vickey, 'that you're still carrying the chicken. It's heavy, but you're strong. Don't let your father down. Keep going, don't drop it. Don't give in. There's only a little way to go now. Hold on.'

'We're all very proud of you,' whispered Sinnéad. 'You haven't far to go. You're still walking, still carrying the chicken. Vickey and I are with you now. We're trotting along beside you, giving you support. Don't give in. Don't drop it . . .'

It seemed an eternity before Old Sage Brush arrived. 'How is she?' he asked.

'Still awake,' said Sinnéad. 'But very weak.'

'Keep talking to her,' said the old fox, and turning to the dog foxes told them, 'Now, here's what I want you to do. Can you find some rotten meat?'

'Hop-along,' suggested Black Tip. 'He buries food whenever he has any to spare.'

'All right. But we haven't much time. Get the most revolting piece of meat you can find and bring it here.'

Black Tip and Skulking Dog immediately raced up to the blackthorns where they alerted Hop-along and She-la to their plight. Hop-along wasted no time. Because of his handicap he was forced to store food more often than other foxes, and sometimes he left it too long. He pointed out several places he used, and they all began scraping furiously to try and find a carcase.

Skulking Dog was the first to come upon one, and as the others crowded around, he closed his eyes and turned his head away, saying, 'Whew Hop-along, you must have forgotten about this one. It's rotten.'

'Well, that's what Old Sage Brush wants,' said Black Tip. 'Come on, let's go.'

'Hop-along and She-la could get the whiff of the rotten

carcase long after they had left, and they just hoped that whatever the old fox had in mind, it would work.

Skulking Dog dropped the carcase at the feet of Old Sage Brush and turned away to get some fresh air.   'It's enough to make you sick,' he gasped.

'That's the whole idea,' said the old fox.   'Now we must make Twinkle eat it.'

She's nearly asleep,' Sinnéad told him.

'Make her eat it,' he repeated firmly.

Seeing what the old fox was at, Skulking Dog overcame his queasiness and took the meat over to Twinkle.

'Come on,' Sinnéad urged her, 'eat this, it'll help you.'

Twinkle groaned and moved her head away from the meat.

It's no use,' said Sinnéad, 'she won't touch it.'

'Then force it into her,' said the old fox.

'But how?'

'You've seen a bird feeding its young haven't you?   Do it the same way.'

Sinnéad took a mouthful of the rotten meat.   Her stomach convulsed slightly, so strong was the stench, but she persevered, and pressing her muzzle into Twinkle's mouth, forced the meat down her throat.

'Now, close her jaws and hold them tight,' ordered the old fox.

This, Skulking Dog proceeded to do, and with her jaws closed, Twinkle had to swallow.

'Now, do it again,' said the old fox.

Twice more they forced Twinkle to swallow mouthfuls of the rotten meat.   Then they all stood back and waited. Twinkle opened her eyes and closed them again.   She groaned and her stomach began to heave.

'Put the rest of it over where she can smell it,' said the old fox.

Picking up the remains of the carcase, Skulking Dog placed it just under her nose.   Immediately her stomach began to heave again, and this time it kept heaving until she had brought up both the rotten meat and the poisoned chicken.

Skulking Dog lay down.   'I feel as bad as she does now,' he groaned.

'Serves you right,' Old Sage Brush told him.   'You should

have known better. If you think the trapper is going to leave food around for a fox, you've another thing coming. That's an old trick of his, and you should have read the signs.' He paused, then added, 'Anyway, Twinkle will be all right now and that's the main thing, but you want to be more careful. She's the only grand-daughter I have.'

Sinnéad thanked the old fox, but he told her there was no need.

'We were wondering,' she added, 'if you might give her the benefit of your wisdom. And maybe the other cubs. You know, the way you did with us.'

'It doesn't seem to have done any of you much good,' he replied.

'Still,' said Vickey, 'we all make mistakes.'

The old fox smiled. Vickey was always the one to put a dog fox in his place, even himself. 'True,' he said, 'and I must admit I've made my share of them, otherwise I wouldn't be blind. All right, as soon as Twinkle is back on her feet, bring them over. I suppose it's time.'

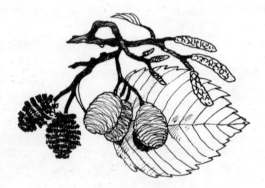

4: A Time to Heal

THE HAWTHORN HEDGES were still snow-white with blossoms, and fragile fronds of cow parsley had spread along the ditches to give them a collar of lace.   Poppies had come up to splash the countryside with crimson, and charlock was giving a yellow tinge to the fields of barley and wheat.   The grain crops, sown in winter to give them an early start, were now like fields of long lush grass, providing cover for many creatures of the wild.   They were also giving cover to the cubs as they made their way to the bog where Old Sage Brush lived.

Hop-along and She-la had agreed to send their cubs now that Sinnéad and Skulking Dog had decided to send Twinkle, and Black Tip and Vickey were sending theirs. The five cubs had been despatched with the gravest of warnings to behave themselves, and to be on the alert for danger.   The whole idea was to try and make them feel independent and more responsible, but of course their parents had no intention of letting them go on their own. Black Tip and Vickey were keeping an eye on them from a discreet distance, and the others weren't far away.

Feeling free and in high spirits, the cubs made their way slowly through the fields.   They were in no hurry.   The sun was shining, the warm summer air was full of exciting scents and sounds, and with all the time in the world to play, that's exactly what they did.

Watching their frolics, Black Tip and Vickey gave each other a knowing look and wondered if they would ever reach the bog.   It seemed to them that the cubs had already forgotten where they were going.   But then, they thought, what was the hurry?   And so they patiently followed their slow and at times erratic progress through the fields.

Being the biggest, it seemed only natural to Young Black Tip that he should be the leader, an assumption that led to many bouts of rough and tumble, not to mention chases which sent them round in circles and sometimes made the two older foxes wonder if they were heading back to Beech Paw.

Vickey smiled.   'It's like taking one step forward and two back.'

Black Tip nodded.   'Maybe when they get hungry they'll move a bit faster.'

Young Black Tip, in fact, was already getting hungry, and on spotting a flock of rooks feeding on newly-cut grass beyond the next hedge, told the others to wait while he went to hunt.

Scab sat down and began to scratch himself, and Twinkle, who was only just recovering from the effects of the poisoned chicken, lay down beside him. Curious to know what Young Black Tip was going to do, Little Running Fox and Scat craned their necks and watched him through the hedge.

A sward of grass had been cut down the field, and the rooks were dotted along this lighter-coloured strip like sloes on a blackthorn bush. Young Black Tip reckoned that if he crept through the long grass, he could take them unawares. He almost succeeded too, but when he pounced, they burst into flight and his intended victim escaped.

His parents, who were watching from a nearby hill, thought he had done very well.   However, his next move was less worthy of admiration.

As the rooks swirled away across the fields in search of a safer place to feed, Young Black Tip spotted a field mouse at the edge of the sward.   It had been sitting there nibbling when he sailed over its head and landed on the newly-cut sward.   Leaning back on its long tail, it stared, mesmerised for a moment, its big eyes and ears clearly expressing surprise.   Then it turned and bounded into the long grass.

Young Black Tip was on it in a flash, and seizing it by the tail, went triumphantly back to the others.   To his surprise,

Scat and Little Running Fox laughed, and he could see smiles breaking out on the faces of Twinkle and Scab.   Dropping his catch on the grass, he asked them what was so funny.

Scat sniggered, saying, 'You won't get very fat on that.'

Looking down, Young Black Tip was amazed to see that all he had returned with was part of the mouse's tail! He couldn't understand it, and felt an awful fool.   Anxious to retrieve the mouse, and his reputation, he dashed back through the hedge and began searching furiously in the long grass.

From their vantage point on the hill, Black Tip and Vickey watched his antics.   They couldn't make out what he was doing, but now they could see something else.   Over the brow of the field where he was rushing about, a tractor had appeared, cutting the grass and spewing it out of a long tube into a high-sided trailer.

Realising that her dog cub was now in serious danger of being cut up and spewed into the same trailer, Vickey barked an urgent warning.   However, she knew he was too far away to hear her, and as Black Tip raced to the rescue she also knew he couldn't possibly reach him in time.

Fortunately Scat was still watching too, and seeing what was about to happen, hopped through the hedge, sped across the grass and hurled himself at Young Black Tip with all the force he could muster.   Both went tumbling through the long grass, and to her great relief Vickey saw them getting up and streaking towards the far hedge.   So intently was the man on the tractor watching the machine behind him, that he didn't even see what had happened.

Once more Black Tip and Vickey admonished the cubs for not taking more care.

'If you are to travel on your own,' said Vickey, 'you must learn to use all your senses.   Your eyes — and your nose — should have told you the grass had just been cut, and your ears should have told you man wasn't far away.'

'Anyway, I almost caught a crow,' Young Black Tip told them.

'And he did catch a mouse,' said his sister, 'only it got away.'

Their parents had to smile when they heard what had happened.

'Well, now you know,' said Vickey. 'You can't catch a field mouse by the tail.'

Scab stopped scratching. 'Why not?'

'Because it jumps out of its skin, that's why,' Vickey told him.

'You mean, all of it?' asked Twinkle.

'Of course not,' said Vickey. 'Just where it's caught by the tail.'

Young Black Tip looked up. 'So that's why I ended up with the skin of its tail. Well that's the best one I ever heard.'

It was the funniest thing the other cubs had heard too, and when they laughed again it wasn't at Young Black Tip, but at their own ignorance and the thought of a mouse jumping out of its skin!

Scat now felt he had earned the right to take the lead. A grateful Black Tip and Vickey agreed, and off they went.

A short time later, Skulking Dog and Sinnéad caught up with Black Tip and Vickey, and they also laughed heartily when they heard what had happened. At the same time, the incident illustrated the dangers the cubs were likely to encounter.

'We'll keep an eye on them now, if you like,' offered Sinnead. 'Maybe you'd like to hunt.'

'Good idea,' said Vickey. 'We could do with a break, and anyway, it doesn't look as if they're going to catch anything for themselves. We'll join you later.'

When Skulking Dog and Sinnéad caught up with the cubs they were in the depths of a wheat field. They couldn't see them, but they could tell by their scent and the occasional movement of the long grass-like crop that they were there. Realising that they would have to be patient, they waited . . . and waited . . . and waited.

'What can they do doing?' wondered Sinnéad.

'Only Vulpes knows,' sighed Skulking Dog. They waited a while longer, and he added, 'Unless they've found another field mouse.'

'But surely it doesn't take five of them to catch a mouse.'

'You wouldn't know, the way they hunt.'

Sinnéad smiled. 'Still, they've been in there a long time. Do you think we should go in and see what they're up to?'

'Leave them be,' said Skulking Dog. 'What harm can they come to?'

They waited another while, watching the wheat and wondering what was going on.

At long last Sinnéad got up. 'I'm not waiting any longer. They should have been out of there long ago.'

Skulking Dog agreed. 'It's strange all right. We better see what they're up to.'

Quietly they stole in through the green stalks of young wheat, and by making their way along the rows which had been sown evenly by man's machines, they crept up on the unsuspecting cubs.

'What are you doing?' asked Sinnéad.

Startled, the cubs looked around.

'Shhhuuu. . .' whispered Twinkle. 'It's man.'

'Where?' asked Skulking Dog.

'Up ahead,' Scab told him. 'He's been watching us for a long time.'

'I think he's waiting for us to break cover,' said Scat.

Skulking Dog was surprised. 'I didn't see him, and I didn't get his scent.'

Young Black Tip sniffed the air. 'That's what I said. But he's there all right.'

'Where is he?' asked Sinnéad. 'Show me.'

Little Running Fox pointed with her nose, saying, 'Over there.'

Slowly Sinnéad raised her head to have a look. Then she stood up and laughed. Skulking Dog also stood up, and seeing that they were in no danger, the cubs followed suit. Ahead of them the figure that had kept them pinned down for so long stood staring, arms outstretched as if to catch them, but didn't move.

Skulking Dog was laughing now too. 'That's not man,' he told them.

'But it looks like man!' said Twinkle. 'What is it?'

Her father was still smiling. 'It's just a figure man makes in his own image — to scare off crows.'

'And he'd be delighted if he knew he had scared you too,' said Sinnéad. 'Still, it's better to be safe than sorry.'

'But how are we to know the difference?' asked Scat.

'Your eyes may deceive you,' said Skulking Dog, 'but not

your nose.   How many times do you have to be told that?'

'Young Black Tip was right,' added Sinnéad. 'You should have known when there was no scent.   You see, all living things have their own peculiar scent — even man. But Old Sage Brush will tell you about it.   He knows more about these things than any of us.   And you better hurry. It's getting late.'

Old Sage Brush was waiting for the cubs at the edge of the bog.   It was getting on towards evening, and the light was fading, but they knew he wasn't depending on the light to find his way.   Telling them to follow closely in his paw-prints, he led them along a maze of paths that took them around seeping turf banks, deep, dark pools of peaty water, and spongy patches of swamp which sagged slightly as they passed.   Sometimes it seemed to them that he had lost his way, but they said nothing, and he led them unerringly to a firm patch of high ground in the middle of the bog.   Covered by silvery birch trees and surrounded by a profusion of young leafy shoots, this island, they found, was dry and secluded and provided a perfect refuge for an unseeing fox who could not risk being seen by man.

Old Sage Brush was highly amused when they told him they had gone fishing only to be caught in the river them-selves, that on the way to the bog they had caught nothing more than a mouse's tail, and how they had been held prisoner in a wheat field by a creature that couldn't move.

He stroked his grey whiskers with the back of his fore-paw and chuckled. 'Well, that's a good one.   Tricked by man and mouse and all in the one day.   I just hope the crows didn't see you.   Or the magpies.   Otherwise we'll never hear the end of it.'

The cubs smiled, and he added, 'Seriously though, you must always be on the alert for danger.   As for fishing, well at least our tails don't come off.'   The cubs wondered what he meant by that, but he didn't explain.   Instead he told them, 'There is a simpler and safer way to catch fish than the way you went about it, and I'll show it to you.   In the mean-time, we must eat.   You stay here.   Don't move and don't make a sound until I come back.'

Darkness had now descended on the bog, and as the old fox left the birches, the cubs wondered how he was going to get enough food for all of them.   In fact, Old Sage Brush had arranged with the older foxes that while the cubs were with him, they would come every so often and leave a cache of food for them at the edge of the bog.   All he would have to do was locate it and bring it back to them.   It took several journeys across the bog before all the cubs were catered for, and when, finally, he settled down with something for himself, they got to talking.

'Why did you choose the bog for your home?'   Young Black Tip wanted to know.

The old fox steadied a leg of cock pheasant with his forepaws, tore off a mouthful of flesh, chewed it slowly and told them, 'To those who do not know the bog, it is a place of many dangers.   But if you know it well, the dangers can give you safety.'   He nibbled at the pheasant leg again, licked his lips and added, 'Let me put it this way.   When the days grow shorter and the dew comes upon the grass, you will see many spiders' webs on the hedgerows.'

'What has that got to do with it?' asked Twinkle.

'Everything,' he told her.   He chewed on his food and swallowed before continuing, 'You see, my little one, the spider is a great hunter.   It will stay in the centre of its web, but it will not be caught in it.   It will come and go as it pleases for it has made many paths for itself.   Yet they are paths no others can travel.   For others they are a trap, but for the spider they are a source of food and a way of escape. So also is this bog and the birches in which you lie.'

Realising that they were in the presence of one who was indeed very wise, the cubs munched away at their own food and listened.

'Because the birches can be seen so clearly,' the old fox went on, 'man seldom sees them.'

'And what happens when he does?' asked Scab.

'Because the bog is full of pitfalls, I can hear danger long before it approaches, and because it is full of paths, I can slip away long before it comes.'

'And how do you manage for food?' asked Scat.

'The bog is full of food, if you know where to look for it. And when others look for it, this is where it comes.   When that happens, all I have to do is wait.'

The old fox made it all sound so very simple, but like

everything he said, the cubs found they had to think about it.   It was the same when Twinkle asked him if all foxes had to learn to be cunning.

Lifting his nose into a gentle breeze which rustled the leaves on the birch trees, he told her, 'All can.'   He paused, before saying, 'Some should.'   And then added, 'None must.'

'When will you show us how to cross the bog?' asked Little Running Fox.   'You know, the way you can cross it, even at night.'

'Soon,' he told her.   'But you must learn to walk with your eyes open before you can walk with them closed.'

Old Sage Brush was as good as his word.   Next morning he took the cubs out of the birches, one at a time, and while their parents kept a look-out for danger in the fields surrounding the bog, he showed them some of the secret ways by which to cross it.

Having done that he told them to memorise every hump and hollow, every pool and wet patch, every twist and turn. Then, when he was satisfied that they were sufficiently familiar with them, he made them count the number of steps it took to reach each point on the paths, and to memorise them.

This they did, and the following day he told them he wanted them to cross the bog again – this time with their eyes closed.   Sensing that they were looking at one another in such a way as to say he must be joking, he said, 'Don't worry.   I'll put down scent markings at certain points along the path.   All you have to do is remember how far you have to go, and where you have to turn.   If you forget, just follow your nose; you'll be all right.'

When Old Sage Brush had gone to get the fox paths ready, Twinkle closed her eyes and cautiously felt her way around.   After a few steps she bumped into a birch tree, and Little Running Fox asked, 'Well, what do you think?'

'I think it must be very frightening to be blind,' Twinkle replied.   She closed her eyes and tried again.

The dog cubs who were lying nearby, stopped talking and watched her.   This time she avoided the trees, but tripped over Young Black Tip's legs and fell head-over-heels.

'That's not fair,' she said.   'You kept quiet on purpose.'

The dog cubs laughed, and Scat told her, 'It's just as well you weren't out in the middle of the bog.'

Twinkle picked herself up and rejoined Running Fox who asked her, 'Are you all right?'

She nodded. 'But he's right you know. If I had been out there I could have ended up in a bog hole.'

Young Black Tip stood up and looked out to see if there was any sign of Old Sage Brush. 'I don't know why he wants us to do it with our eyes closed anyway. It would be much easier to do it by the light of gloomglow.'

Scat agreed. 'This is just pretending.'

Scab scratched himself vigorously and said, 'Well, he seems to know what he's doing.'

Young Black Tip was still looking out through the screen of young birch shoots when Old Sage Brush slipped in through the other side. 'All right,' he smiled, 'let's get on with it. Young Black Tip, you seem anxious to be on your way. Off you go now, and keep your eyes closed. Scat, you keep close behind him. Keep your eyes on him and warn him if he's going wrong.'

In spite of the brashness of his manner, the two she-cubs could not help but admire Young Black Tip as he picked his way through the bog. They kept Old Sage Brush informed of his every move, and when he returned the old fox nodded. He seemed well pleased.

After that, Young Black Tip kept an eye on Scat, Scat kept an eye on Scab, and the two vixens kept an eye on each other. Not one of them put a paw wrong, and when they lay down beneath the birches to rest and have something to eat, the old fox told them they had all done well.

Delighted with themselves, the cubs frolicked and played and when they gathered around once more, Old Sage Brush told them, 'Now it's time to try it on your own.'

'On our own?' asked Young Black Tip. 'But the scent has gone cold.'

'I know,' the old fox replied, 'but when you tread the fox-path of life you will be on your own, except at breeding time, and there will be no one to mark the pitfalls along the way. Now off you go, and be careful. If I can do it, so can you.'

So it was that the cubs spent the rest of the day picking

their way across the bog, on their own and with their eyes closed. There were moments when they were afraid, times when they were unsure which way to turn, and even occasions when their next step might have been their last. However, they all came through it safely, and by evening felt they had mastered not only the bog but their own fears.

'Now,' said the old fox, 'comes the difficult part.'

The cubs looked at one another, and Little Running Fox asked, 'But what can be more difficult than crossing a bog with our eyes closed?'

'Crossing it in the dark,' the old fox told her, 'with your eyes open.'

'I don't understand,' said Scat. 'How can that be?'

Old Sage Brush curled his tail around his frail body and lowered his head on to it. 'That is something you must discover for yourselves,' he said. 'Scab, you will stay here with me. I don't want the wounds on your body to get dirty. The rest of you go over to the edge of the bog while it is still light. Find the food your parents have left for you, and bring it back when it is dark, not before. When you return it will be time for you to leave.'

Slipping out through the young shoots of birch, the cubs followed one of the paths across the bog which had now become so familiar to them.

'What does he mean, when we return it will be time for us to leave?' asked Twinkle.

They were walking nose-to-tail behind Young Black Tip.

'I don't know,' said Scat.

'And what does he mean when he says it's more difficult to cross the bog with our eyes open?' wondered Little Running Fox.

'He has a strange way of putting things all right,' said her brother. 'I'd rather cross the bog at night with my eyes open, than cross it in the day with my eyes closed.'

The others agreed. They crossed on to the firm ground at the edge of the bog without too much difficulty, and began nosing around for the food which they knew was buried there.

Darkness had fallen on the bog, and beneath the birches Old Sage Brush dozed.   Nearby, Scab sat and watched him.

Itching as always, he scratched himself again and thought how tired the old fox must be.   Yet in all the times he had criss-crossed the bog to help them get to know it, he had never once complained.   His concern was for them — all of them — and Scab couldn't help thinking that Twinkle was lucky to have such a wise fox as her grandfather.   But then, he thought, they were all lucky.

Time passed and there was still no sign of the others returning.   Scab began to feel uneasy, and with Old Sage Brush asleep he also began to feel lonely.   He had told himself he wouldn't disturb the old fox, but now as the breeze whispered through the birch leaves, it seemed to him that he was the only one left on the bog.

'Sage Brush,' he said quietly.   'Sage Brush.'

'What is it Scab?'

'They're not back yet.'

The old fox lifted his head.   'Can you see anything?'

Scab nipped out of the birches and returned almost immediately to tell him, 'There's a strange sort of light on the bog.'

'Just as I thought.'

Scab waited for an explanation, but Old Sage Brush didn't give him one.   Instead he put his head down again and went to sleep.   Curious to know what was going on, Scab went out to have another look at the bog.   The strange light was still there, and he wondered if the others had seen it. . .

In fact, the strange light was the reason why the others hadn't returned.   Its appearance up ahead gave them a considerable shock, for they immediately assumed it was something to do with man.   They had no way of knowing that it was caused by a luminous gas that rose from the bog, and that because of its elusive nature, man called it the 'will-o'-the-wisp'.

Scat was leading them back when he saw it, and he was so taken aback by it that he almost dropped the dead chicken he was carrying.

Young Black Tip had a pheasant in his mouth, and putting it down, he asked, 'What is it?'

'It must be the trapper,' whispered Twinkle.   'When I was

recovering from his poison my mother warned me that he sometimes shines lights to trap us.'

'How can that trap us?' asked Scat.

'She said he makes the noise of a fox or a trapped rabbit. My father got shot once when he answered such a call.'

Scat was surprised.   'Skulking Dog?'

Twinkle nodded, and Little Running Fox said, 'That's right. My mother told me my father was out hunting with Skulking Dog at the time.   Skulking Dog thought it was a vixen calling, but when he followed the sound, man shone a light into his eyes and shot him.'

'He was wounded,' Twinkle went on, 'but Black Tip helped him to get away.'

Young Black Tip's ears turned this way and that as he listened intently to the sounds of the night.   'But I don't hear any noise like that.'

'Still,' said Scat, 'I think we better keep clear of it, whatever it is.   If we cut across we can get to another fox path which will take us around it.'

'Do you think that's wise?' asked Little Running Fox.

'I think we know the bog well enough by now,' replied Scat.

Young Black Tip agreed.   The two vixen cubs weren't so sure it was the right thing to do, but when Scat turned off the path away from the light, and Young Black Tip followed, they went too.

Finding the other path, however, wasn't as easy as Scat imagined.   When he came to a path which looked as if it might lead somewhere, it invariably ended in a bog hole or at a turf bank that dropped sharply into the darkness.

Each time they retraced their steps for a short distance and tried again, but try as they would, they continued to go astray.   Several times Scat found himself up to his knees in dark, foul-smelling water.   Once he slipped into a pool and the others had to drag him out.   And even though the others were following him, they had narrow escapes too.   If they turned to try another way by themselves, or simply didn't keep in line, an empty step would send them tumbling into the mud or water.   To make matters worse, the strange light was still as close to them as ever.

Not knowing what to do or where to turn, they stopped to

consider their situation once more.

'Do you think he's watching us?' asked Little Running Fox.

'I don't think it is the trapper,' said Twinkle.

'What then?'

'I think it's a star.'

'But the stars are high in the sky.   That's low in the bog.'

'Still,' said Twinkle.   'It was from the stars that I got my name.   My mother told me that one day they would show me the way.'

Little Running Fox was still staring at the strange light. 'Our parents told us that too.   But do you think this is what they meant?'

'I don't know, but maybe we should follow it and see.'

'But how can we follow it?' asked Young Black Tip.   'Even if we wanted to.   Sure we can hardly move without taking a wrong step.'

They were all wet and dirty now, and sensing that they were also getting tired, Scat said, 'All right, let's try and get back to the path we were on.'

By following their scents, they did eventually succeed in returning to the path they had left.   The strange light was still ahead of them, but bearing in mind what Twinkle had said, they decided to go towards it.   However, as they did so, a peculiar thing happened.   They found themselves straying off into unknown parts of the bog again.   It was almost as if the light was luring them away from the path. And when they found it again, they could see they were making very little progress towards either the light or the birches.

Exhausted, they lay down in a patch of heather and wondered what to do.   Twinkle was very disappointed.   'It doesn't seem to be a star after all,' she said.   'What are we going to do now?'

'Maybe we should wait until morning,' suggested Scat.

'Or try and get back out onto firm ground,' said Young Black Tip.

'Somehow,' his sister told him, 'I think Old Sage Brush expects us to make it across to the birches tonight.'

Scat nodded.   'You're probably right.   And he did say it would be difficult.'

Little Running Fox was trying to recall what the old fox

had said. 'What was it now? He said it could be more difficult crossing the bog with our eyes open than with them closed. Maybe that's the answer.'

'What is?' asked Young Black Tip.

'Maybe Old Sage Brush knows about the strange light,' she said. 'Maybe he knows that it leads you astray.'

'So?' Scat was as puzzled as any of them.

'So he was telling us that we should close our eyes and ignore it.'

'The way he has taught us to do,' exclaimed Twinkle.

Without waiting to hear what the dog cubs thought of her idea, Little Running Fox picked up her food, and closing her eyes, followed the path just the way they had done during the day. Not to be outdone, the others did likewise, and a short time later they were all back at the birches.

'How did you get past the light?' asked Scab in surprise.

'What light?' asked Little Running Fox.

'That light out there on the bog.'

'We saw no light,' said Twinkle, and turning to the others, asked, 'Did we?'

Young Black Tip and Scat shook their heads.

'Then what took you so long?' asked Scab. 'And how come you're in such a mess?'

'We did see it all right,' Little Running Fox told him. 'But I suppose you could say we turned a blind eye to it. We thought maybe Sage Brush could tell us what it was.'

The old fox smiled. 'I'll tell you about it later. But you have done well. And you didn't even lose the food. Now, make good use of it. Tomorrow we leave the bog and go out into the world of man.'

5: A Time to Laugh

A GENTLE BREEZE was plucking petals from the hawthorns and scattering them in the fields like flakes of snow as Old Sage Brush and the cubs made their way along the hedgerows towards the river. The petals fell so softly that the old fox could not hear them. However, he could feel them on his face and remember how beautiful they used to be. He could hear the small birds singing, and the rustle of the unripe barley as its slender spikes reached for the sun and combed the warm summer air. As they trotted along, he could also hear the other cubs telling Scab how they had made their way past the strange light they had seen on the bog.

Scab, who was leading the way, stopped and asked, 'But what was it?'

They were at the corner of a field, and Old Sage Brush lay down among the weeds to get his breath back. The others lay down beside him and he told them, 'It can be very frightening all right – until you learn to ignore it.'

'But what is it?' asked Twinkle.

'It's just something that comes from the bog,' said the old fox. 'A little trick nature plays on us. They say it has sometimes led man astray too.'

'I thought it might be a star,' Twinkle confessed. 'That's why we tried to follow it.'

The old fox smiled and told her, 'The only stars you must follow are those of the Great Running Fox in the Sky. It is the guiding light of all foxes.'

'When will we see it?' asked Little Running Fox.

'When the ground grows hard and the sky grows cold,' replied the old fox. 'It will wait up there until it is time for you to strike out on your own, and then it will show you the way.'

'How will we know when that time has come?' asked Young Black Tip.

Old Sage Brush raised his nose to sniff the breeze, and said, 'You'll know.'

'But how?' Scat wanted to know.

'How does the young bird know when it is time to leave the nest?' the old fox asked. 'How does the new butterfly know when it is time to spread its wings? How does the young frog know when it is time to take its first leap into the long grass? Even the sycamore seed knows when to spin to earth and put down its own roots.'

Like so many things the old fox said, he had posed questions to which he did not expect an answer, which was just as well. The cubs didn't know what the answer was, but they now knew it was something that would take care of itself.

There was no sign of their parents as they passed through Beech Paw, although they sensed they weren't far away, and a short time later they arrived at the river beyond the dam.

'You should have done what Ratwiddle told you,' said Old Sage Brush. 'You should always keep a look-out for danger.'

'It's so difficult to know what he means,' said Twinkle.

The old fox nodded. 'I suppose it is.'

'Anyway, how can we keep an eye on the dam and fish at the same time?' asked Scat.

'There is a way,' the old fox told him. 'But the first thing to remember is that you won't catch any fish by charging into the water. They're too fast. You must stalk them, just the way you stalk any prey. Now Scab, take me over to the bank, and crawl on your belly so the fish won't see you.'

Together, the two of them crawled through the grass until they were at the river's edge, and at a given signal, the others followed.

'It is important,' whispered the old fox, 'that you should not talk, otherwise the fish will hear you. And you must avoid throwing shadows on the water, or they will see you.'

The cubs were listening and wondering. They couldn't figure out how they were going to catch any fish if they couldn't go in after them, couldn't make any noise, and couldn't be seen!

'Are the small fish still there?' asked the old fox.

Scab peeped over the bank and told him that the shoal was moving around in the river immediately in front of them.

Old Sage Brush edged forward until he was able to ease his tail down into the water. Curious to see what he was doing, the cubs shuffled forward and watched.

The old fox allowed his brush to trail in the slow-moving water and a few moments later a strange thing happened. Whether it was the movement of the tail, or the scent it was releasing into the water, the cubs had no way of knowing, but the small fish were attracted to it. Cautiously they swam around the tip. Then one ventured closer and became entangled in the hairs. Feeling the tug on his tail, the old fox whipped it out and landed the fish on the bank.

Taken by surprise, the cubs pounced on the wriggling fish, only to be told to leave it. They could eat it later, when they had more of them. But first they had to catch them, and now it was their turn.

It wasn't long before the cubs were beaming as, one by one, they dangled their tails over the bank and plucked the small fish from the water. It took Scab a little longer than the others, as there weren't many hairs left on his tail to either tempt or catch anything. However, he eventually caught one, and after landing it gave way to the impatience of the others and lay back and watched. He could see they were having great fun.

'Sage Brush,' he said after a while.

'What?' asked the old fox who was dozing in the sun.

'This itch of mine. Do you think it will go away?'

The old fox didn't answer for a moment. He had seen many a fox with an itch. Some had lived, others had died, but he didn't want to say that to Scab. Instead, he told him, 'Well, no itch is so serious as to be despaired of, but none is so trivial as to be made light of.'

'What can I do to stop it?'

'It all depends on what's causing it.' The old fox thought

for a moment. 'There is one thing that might help you. It's a flower that grows on the bog. If only I could see, I could find it for you.'

'There's nothing wrong with my eyes. Maybe I could find it if you described it to me.'

'Very well. As soon as we return to the bog we'll see if it has come into bloom yet. In the meantime, try not to scratch, keep your wounds clean and try not to pass it on to the others.'

Feeling somewhat comforted by the old fox's words, Scab turned to watch the others again, and smiled when he saw how much they were enjoying themselves.

A short time later, Black Tip and Vickey arrived with some food. By this time the cubs had devoured the small fish they had caught, but this had only whetted their appetite, and they tore into the food with disgusting enthusiasm.

'Well Sage Brush,' asked Vickey, 'how are they doing?'

'Fine,' said the old fox, and he told them what he had taught them so far.

'I remember once you told us that ducks only lay in the morning,' Black Tip recalled, 'and it was news to us. Maybe you could tell them a bit about that sort of thing. Who knows, we might learn something too.'

The old fox smiled. 'What made you think of that?'

'We saw a pheasant's nest on the way down,' Vickey told him, 'but the egg shells were empty.'

Having stuffed themselves as usual, the cubs were lying listening.

'You will find,' the old fox told them, 'that many birds lay in the morning. Some small birds, like finches and wrens, lay at sunrise, but you'll be more interested in the bigger birds. Now, as Black Tip has said, ducks usually lay in the morning too. Others, like pigeons and pheasants, lay later in the day. However, ducks and pheasants both make their nests on the ground, so you shouldn't have too much difficulty finding out if they have laid or not – provided, of course, something else hasn't found the nest first.'

The cubs smiled, and he went on, 'But then, if something else has found it, that can be your meal instead.'

'Like what?' asked Scat.

'Like a crow, or a hedgehog.'

'But how will we know what has been at it?' asked Little Running Fox.

'By the way the shells have been broken,' the old fox told her. 'You see, every creature has its own way of doing things, and if you know what to look for, the broken shells will give you a good idea what it was.'

Sensing that they were waiting to hear more, he explained, 'The signs can vary, of course. But the grey crow or magpie will peck a hole in the egg, then put in the upper part of its beak, lift it up and drink it. The hedgehog will bite a large hole in the egg and lick out the yolk with its tongue – but you'll have no trouble knowing when it has been around. It might leave a few shallow shells behind it, but generally the shells are in bits and the nest is in a terrible mess. Now the stoat – it's different again. It will take the eggs away and eat them somewhere else. But while we will crush an egg in our mouths, the stoat will bite a small hole in the end of it and get at the yolk that way.'

'It all sounds very complicated,' said Twinkle.

'Maybe it does,' said the old fox, 'but you'll get to know the signs. Now Vickey, show me this pheasant's nest you saw on the way down, and let's see if we can figure out what has been at it.'

The nest was at the base of a thick hedge, and the cubs crawled in so that they could get a close look at it.

'Well,' said the old fox, 'what do you see?'

'All the shells are broken,' Scab told him.

'And there's not a thing left in them,' observed Young Black Tip.

Twinkle sniffed at the nest, and said, 'There's no scent, so it must have happened a while ago.'

'Tell me about the shells,' said the old fox. 'They hold the clue.'

'They've been broken in half,' Twinkle told him.

'And some of them are tucked inside each other,' added Little Running Fox.

'Are the broken edges pointing in?'

'Some of them,' said Twinkle. 'What does that mean?'

'It means,'' replied the old fox, 'that they weren't eaten.'

The cubs were still looking at the broken shells, and seeing their puzzled looks, Black Tip and Vickey smiled.

'But if they weren't eaten,' concluded Scat, 'that means they . . .'

'That's right,' said the old fox.   'They hatched out.   You see, the chicks peck around the shells from the inside until they break them open, and sometimes their movements make the two parts of the shells slip inside one another.'

The cubs could see that now, but they wondered how the old fox knew all these things.   They had never seen chicks breaking eggs, not to mention crows, hedgehogs or stoats. And even now as they thought about it, it never occurred to them how such a small animal as a stoat could take something as big as a duck egg or a pheasant egg, back to its den.   However, it wasn't long before they were to find out.

They were returning to the bog by way of Beech Paw.   Little Running Fox was a short distance ahead with her parents, while the other cubs trotted alongside Old Sage Brush asking him questions and listening intently to what he had to say.   It was obvious to Black Tip and Vickey that the cubs' admiration for the old fox was growing.   So also was their own admiration for Young Black Tip and Little Running Fox, as they thought they could already see in them certain qualities which they felt they themselves possessed.

For her part, Little Running Fox felt very grown-up to be allowed to lead the way, and when, emerging from a hedge, she spotted a stoat loping along a cow track, it didn't occur to her that she should ask her parents what to do.   She had seen a stoat before, of course, but to her amazement this one was trundling an egg along the track with its nose, and even though it was going quite fast, the egg was still in one piece! Acting on instinct, she immediately dashed across in front of it and without stopping, took the egg from under its nose. Then, eating the egg as she ran, she returned to her parents, licking her lips and feeling quite pleased with herself.

Her parents, however, were far from pleased.   The egg, they could see, was gone, but the stoat was still there.

'You shouldn't have done that,' said Black Tip.

Little Running Fox looked up.   She was still smiling. 'Why not?'

Vickey was watching the stoat intently.   'Because it won't leave us alone until it gets the egg back.'

Little Running Fox laughed. 'But it can't get it back. I've eaten it.'

'I know,' said Vickey.   'That's the problem.'

Old Sage Brush and the other cubs had almost caught up and were preparing to come through the hedge to join them. Sensing that they had stopped, he paused and inquired, 'What's wrong?'

Vickey told him, and he asked, 'How many are there?'

'One, maybe two,' replied Vickey.

'I think there's more,' said Little Running Fox.   'Look, there, there, and there.'

Peering through the hedge, the other cubs thought she must be right, for every now and then they could see the flash of a small white throat popping up out of the under-growth at the bottom of the far hedge.

'No,' said Black Tip, 'there's only one.   It's peeping up here and there to keep an eye on us.   That's the way they do it.'

'Then why don't we go after it?' asked Young Black Tip.

'Because it's too small,' said Old Sage Brush.   'It can follow us to earth, but we cannot follow it.   That is why the

stoat is always a hunter, rarely the hunted.' He paused. 'It might also whistle up its friends to help it, and that's a fight we can do without.'

'But we don't mind a fight,' said Scat, 'no matter how many of them there are.'

Old Sage Brush smiled. 'I know that. But at the moment you're too young, and I'm too old.'

Vickey still hadn't taken her eye off the small, snake-like creature that continued to watch them from the far hedge. 'What do you think we should do then?' she asked. 'If we go to Beech Paw, we'll only draw them on to Hop-along and the others , and if we go with you, we'll only lead them to your hiding place on the bog.'

Old Sage Brush was silent, and Scab said, 'But they'd never find the pathways across the bog.'

'Maybe not,' said Old Sage Brush, 'but then they wouldn't need to find them. They're too light and too fast. The bog would be no obstacle to them.'

The stoat was still sticking its small head up every now and then to see what they were going to do. Black Tip turned and walked back a few paces so that he could lie down close to the old fox. 'There's still only one of them,' he whispered through the hedge. 'It hasn't seen you yet, so it doesn't know you're here. If you take the cubs back to the bog, we'll stay here and try and figure out what to do.'

Vickey came closer too and told the old fox, 'Black Tip's right. It's our problem and we'll have to deal with it.'

'What about Running Fox?' asked Young Black Tip. 'Can she come too?'

Vickey shook her head. 'She's the one it has its eye on.'

'Then I'll stay and help her.'

Vickey smiled, but shook her head once more. 'No, you go with Sage Brush. We don't know how many stoats we may have to face, and if we can't cope with them, your strength may be needed on the bog.'

'Your mother's right,' said Black Tip. 'If they find their way to the bog Sage Brush will need all the help he can get. And don't worry, it's not the first time we've faced a stoat.'

'True,' said Old Sage Brush, 'and perhaps it's time you passed on some of your experience to your daughter. Remember, if you teach the stoat a lesson, it is Little

Running Fox who will learn it.'

'That's easier said than done,' replied Black Tip.   'Stoats may be small but they're fearless fighters.'

'Maybe so,' said the old fox, 'but as I've told you before, courage is no substitute for cunning.'

Black Tip nodded, and turning to Scab the old fox said, 'Come now, we've no time to lose.'

6: A Time to Weep

AS OLD SAGE BRUSH and the other three cubs slipped away to return to the bog by another route, Black Tip and Vickey rejoined their daughter and wondered what to do about the stoat. It was still watching them from the far hedge, and after a while Little Running Fox said, 'Why don't we just out-run it?'

'Because this is our territory,' Vickey told her, 'and we must let nothing drive us from it.'

Little Running Fox looked over at the hedge. She was sure there was more than one stoat watching them now. 'But it was only an egg,' she protested. 'Why should they make such a fuss over an egg?'

'Because this is also their territory,' explained Black Tip. 'We have always shared it with them. We don't prey on them, and they don't prey on us.'

'We have never been friends,' added Vickey, 'but we have never been enemies.'

'But I've seen magpies and rooks mob you when you were carrying food back to the earth for us,' said Little Running Fox. 'If it's all right for the birds to try and steal our food, why can't we take it from the stoats?'

'That's different,' Vickey explained. 'We are the enemies of the magpie and the crow. We kill them when we can, and they know that. That's why they try to get us to drop our prey and draw the attention of others to us.'

'But why should we be afraid to run and afraid to fight?'

Black Tip knew he must be patient. 'It is because we are not afraid that we do not run. But it is only because we cannot catch the stoat that we do not fight it.'

'They're like the light you saw on the bog,' said Vickey, 'They're very hard to pin down.'

'They also have a good brain,' said Black Tip.   'Too good for their size, and they're very vengeful.   They'll choose their own time and place and strike when you least expect it.'

'They're like a leech,' continued Vickey.   'If you're not careful you'll waken up to find their teeth in the back of your neck and they won't let go until you are drained of your courage and your life.'

'Still,' said Little Running Fox, 'if there's only one of them, what have we to fear?   There are three of us.'

Vickey looked across at the small head and white throat which kept bobbing up and down in the undergrowth.   'I think there are two of them now, and as Old Sage Brush was saying they sometimes hunt in packs.   We must act quickly – before any more of them come.'

'What are you going to do?' asked Little Running Fox.

Her mother shook her head.   'I don't know.'

'But you said you faced a stoat once before.'

'So we did,' said Black Tip.   'It was on our journey to find the secret of survival.   We came across a large cat and a small dog which hunted stoats.'

'We never found out how they did it,' said Vickey, 'but they just caught them for fun.'

Black Tip nodded.   'They teased them and played with them when they were half dead.'

'They even tried to do the same with me,' Vickey recalled. 'They had me cornered in an earth and I think they would have killed me if it hadn't been for your father.   He lured a stoat to the earth where I was trapped so that they would have something else to play with and leave me alone.'

'How did you lure the stoat?' asked Little Running Fox.

'I took a rabbit from it,' said Black Tip.   'I knew it would follow me until it got it back.'

'Why can't we do the same with this stoat?   All I took was an egg.   Can't we give it one back?'

Vickey thought for a moment.   'We could try, I suppose. What type of egg was it?'

Little Running Fox shook her head.

'Was it a pheasant egg, a hen egg, or a duck egg?' asked Vickey.

'I'm sorry, but I really didn't get a good look at it. All I know is that it was an egg.'

'All right,' said Vickey, 'don't worry. Anyway, it's worth a try. Black Tip, perhaps you would go down to one of the farms and see what you can get — and be careful.'

Black Tip nodded, and Vickey and Little Running Fox stood up so that he could slip away through the hedge unnoticed.

A short time later, Black Tip returned with a hen's egg. Taking care not to break it, Little Running Fox took it and walked over to the cow track where she had taken the one from the stoat.

Black Tip and Vickey watched as she gently placed the egg on the track — and so did the stoats.

Returning to her parents, Little Running Fox also lay down and watched. The stoats, she could see, were curious. Suddenly one of them streaked across to the cow track, sniffed the egg, stood up on its hind legs to have a

closer look at the foxes, and disappeared back into the hedge. 'They didn't take it,' she said.

Black Tip looked at Vickey. 'Maybe it was because our scent was on it.'

Vickey wasn't sure. 'Maybe it was the wrong type of egg. We could try a duck egg. You stay here and I'll see if I can get one.'

Some time later, Vickey returned from the meadows with a duck egg which Little Running Fox placed out on the cow track. Once more one of the stoats darted out to see what she had left, but once more rejected it.

'Maybe,' suggested Black Tip, 'it was a pheasant egg.'

'Do you think you could find one?' asked Vickey.

'If a stoat can find one, so can I,' asserted Black Tip, and off he went. He knew that the pheasants had started laying a while back and that some of the eggs, like the ones they had just seen on the way back from the river, had already hatched out. However, he searched and searched until he found a fairly fresh clutch, and brought one back.

Little Running Fox dutifully took the pheasant egg and placed it out on the cow track. Once again one of the stoats streaked out of the hedge to examine it, but once again left it where it was. And so the foxes and the stoats continued to watch each other . . .

At long last darkness came, and the moon spread its soft light across the fields.

'I think it's time we made a move,' said Black Tip.

'What do you have in mind?' asked Vickey.

'Well, the stoat is small and so are its eyes. Our eyes are large and we can see better than most, especially when we have the wide eye of gloomglow to help us. Perhaps we could strike first while we have the advantage.'

Little Running Fox looked up at the moon, and Vickey nodded, saying, 'Right, but we'll have to tread very carefully.'

Half way across the field, however, they found that they weren't the only ones to think of striking first. Their keen vision detected several stoats creeping through the grass towards them, and whether it was equally keen vision or some other sharp sense that the stoats possessed, they became aware of the foxes at exactly the same time.

Choosing not to fight in the open, they turned and streaked back to the hedge.   The foxes charged after them, but they quickly disappeared into small rat-holes and crevices where they knew they couldn't be followed.

'So much for that,' said Black Tip as they returned to their own hedge.

'Still,' Vickey assured him.   'It was a good idea.   And it's just as well we moved when we did or they'd have been in around our ears.'

Black Tip settled down and scanned the far hedge for any further sign of movement.   'A good idea, but not good enough, and I can't think of anything better.'

'Maybe we should ask Old Sage Brush,' suggested Little Running Fox.   'He might know what to do.'

'We don't want to risk drawing them on to him,' said Vickey.   'Anyway, he wanted us to figure it out for ourselves.'

'What about Ratwiddle then?'

'What about him?' asked Black Tip.

'Well, if he's as good at catching rats as you say he is, maybe he knows how to catch stoats.'

Black Tip thought about the idea for a moment, and Little Running Fox added, 'Unless you think we'd be putting him in danger too.'

'No, I think he'd be safe enough.   Even man knows he's a bit strange and leaves him alone.   Do you think you could find him?'

Little Running Fox nodded and looked at her mother, thinking she would probably object.   However Vickey just smiled and said, 'All right, but whatever you do, don't bring back any of his fleas.   He's got more than his share.'

Anxious to get her parents out of the predicament she had got them into, Little Running Fox sped off towards the river. She found Ratwiddle among the alders — but she didn't find the answer she was looking for.

'I think his mind was up in the sky,' she told her parents when she returned.

'Isn't it always,' sighed Vickey.   'Poor Ratwiddle.   What exactly did he say?'

'He said, what was it now?   He said, even a bird can't bite a mite.'

'What did he mean by that?' wondered Black Tip.

Little Running Fox shook her head.   'And what are mites anyway?'

'I think he was talking about the small parasites birds sometimes get in their feathers,' said Vickey.

'Do you think he was trying to tell me something?'

Vickey nodded.   'Probably — but what?'

'What do birds do when they can't bite these things?' asked Little Running Fox.

'Sometimes they shuffle around in the dust,' said Black Tip.   'Maybe that's how they get rid of them.'

'Old Sage Brush says that in some lands they let ants crawl through their feathers,' said Vickey. 'But I've never seen them do it in the Land of Sinna.'

'Nor I,' said Black Tip.   'What would they do that for anyway?'

'I think he said the ants kill the mites they can't get at themselves.   Dust probably does the same thing.'

Little Running Fox was perplexed.   'But what's that got to do with stoats?'

Vickey got to her feet.   'Now that I think of it, maybe it's got everything to do with it.   I think Ratwiddle was saying the stoats are too small for us to catch, so we must get something small that will get rid of them for us.'

Black Tip got up too.   'But what?'

Vickey was thinking.   'Something that is bigger than stoats, but small enough to go after them.'

'When we go to earth man sometimes uses small dogs to come after us,' said Black Tip.   'But we can't draw them on to the stoats without drawing them on to ourselves.'

'Anyway, they'd be too big to follow the stoats,' said Vickey.

'What does man use when the earths are too small for dogs?' asked Little Running Fox.

'Ferrets,' Black Tip told her.   'They're a bit like mink, only yellow.   He uses them to hunt rabbits.'

Little Running Fox jumped to her feet.   'The mink.   We could use the mink!'

Her parents looked at her in alarm.

'The mink down at the river,' she explained.   'They owe us a favour, remember?'

Black Tip shook his head.   'They'd never do it, not for us.'

'How do you know until you ask?'

'No,' said Vickey.   'It's too dangerous.'

Little Running Fox lowered her head on to her forelegs and her parents could sense that she was close to tears.

'All right,' said Vickey at last, 'I suppose it's worth a try.   But keep your distance from them.   They're every bit as dangerous as stoats, maybe more so.'

Little Running Fox suppressed a sniffle and raced away towards the river again.   She couldn't believe how much trouble she had brought upon her parents and herself by one thoughless act.   As she ran through the night she rebuked herself a thousand times, and hoped that the she-mink would remember what Young Black Tip had done for her cub.   After some searching she found both mother and cub not far from where she had spoken to Ratwiddle.   She also found the same hostility her brother had found. However, despite her hostility, the she-mink acknowledged that Young Black Tip had saved her cub from drowning.

'Does that mean you'll help us?' asked Little Running Fox.

'I would like to,' replied the she-mink, 'but there is a problem.   You see, the stoats are very akin to the mink.   Members of the same family, you might say.   So how can we move against them?'

Little Running Fox was silent.   This was something she hadn't thought of, and she wondered if it was the real reason why her parents had thought she would be wasting her time.

'Now, if it was ferrets,' continued the mink, 'that would be different.   They have deserted our family to become the servants of man.'

'But it's the stoats that are causing us the problem.   And all I did was take an egg.'

The she-mink's hostile face softened into a smile.   'That's the way stoats are.   They never give up.'

'But we've tried to make it up to them,' said Little Running Fox.   'We've given them three eggs, and they won't take one of them.'

'Then you must make them.'

'But how?'

The she-mink shook her head.   'That is something you

must work out for yourselves.   But perhaps I can help you.'

'How?'

'Well, the stoats in that area live in a pile of stones not far away, over by the trapper's house.   If it's any help to you we could drive them back there.'

Little Running Fox's face lit up.   'Oh would you, would you really?   That would be a great help.'

'All right,' said the mink.   'I suppose we owe you that much.   And who knows, perhaps they will leave you alone. If not, you will have to think of some way to make them take the egg.'

Shortly after Little Running Fox had rejoined her parents at the foot of the hedge, they sensed movement in the shadows.   Even with their keen eyesight, they couldn't see anything, but they knew the mink were passing by.   They cocked their ears and listened.   Nothing.   Then the night air was filled with the squeaks and squeals of the stoats as the mink moved into the far hedge after them.   The foxes got to their feet, ready to join in, but there was no need. Suddenly the night was quiet again; they knew the mink had kept their promise, and that the stoats were on their way back to their pile of stones.

Little Running Fox was delighted, and she could see her parents were very pleased with what she had done.

'I didn't think they would do it,' Black Tip told her.

'Nor I,' said Vickey.   'Now the question is, will the stoats stay in the stones, or will they continue to follow us?   We must make sure.'

Black Tip agreed, and so they followed the scent of the stoats and the mink until they came to the pile of stones. There was no sign of life, but they retired to a disused earth, which they found nearby, to wait and see if their nightmare was finally over.

'What do we do if they come after us again?' asked Little Running Fox.

'Don't worry,' Vickey assured her, 'we'll think of something when the time comes — if it comes.'

'And it may not,' said Black Tip.   'They may have had enough by now.   So why don't you two rest.   I'll see if there's anything around here worth catching besides stoats. Then we can eat before we leave.'

Black Tip hadn't noticed until now what a lovely night it was.   The air was warm, a gentle breeze brought him many appetising scents, and the fields were bright and clear in the light of gloomglow.   Not far from the earth he came across a rabbit which was taking advantage of the moonlight and the absence of stoats to come out and nibble the grass.   It hadn't reckoned on a fox being so near the trapper's house, and it paid dearly for its mistake.

As Black Tip carried the rabbit back to the earth, he hoped they were finished with the stoats.   He didn't mind a fight, even a fight with another dog fox, but he found it frustrating to try and fight an enemy he couldn't come to grips with.   If only he could get his teeth into them.   Just once, he thought, that was all it would take.   Little did he realise he was about to get his chance . . .

Arriving back at the earth, he discovered to his horror that while they couldn't find the stoats, the stoats had found them.   In the half-light of dawn, they had made their move, creeping out of the stones and striking at the two vixens shortly after he had left.

Vickey and Little Running Fox had withdrawn from the earth in the face of the onslaught, and the scene he came upon was one of chaos.   With their ears flattened back in fear and anger, the vixens were yikkering and snapping to try and ward off the vicious little creatures which darted in and around them in a determined effort to get at their throats.

Dropping the rabbit, Black Tip immediately joined in the fight, and together they succeeded in driving the stoats back into the pile of stones.

Vickey sank to the ground, exhausted, and Little Running Fox flopped down beside her.

'So they haven't given up yet,' panted Black Tip.

Vickey was still trying to get her breath.

'They're smarter than I thought,' he continued.   'If we turn our backs on them they'll be on us like a flash, and if we stay here the trapper's dogs will find us.'

The sun's rays were already striking the stones and spreading new warmth across the fields.

Vickey nodded.   'They've chosen the time and the place, and both hold great danger for us.'

Little Running Fox said nothing. She was too pre-
occupied trying to soothe a swollen lip.

'Did you get bitten?' asked Vickey.

'No, it's a sting.   I put my nose in where it didn't belong.'

Black Tip laughed, but Vickey inquired, 'Where?'

'Up in the stones.   There's a wasps' nest there as well as
stoats.'

Almost as if she had been stung herself, Vickey jumped to
her feet. 'That's it,' she cried. 'That's it Running Fox.
You've found the answer to Ratwiddle's riddle.   Now,
here's what we're going to do.'

Having explained what she had in mind, Vickey waited
until she and Little Running Fox had got their strength
back.   Then they all got up and made their way slowly
through the fields.   It wasn't long before the stoats emerged
from the stones and followed, but they pretended not to see
them.

When the stoats were well clear of the stones, Black Tip
slipped around behind them and set to work.   Between
most of the stones were soil, grass and other rubble, but
here and there were the holes which the stoats used.
Searching around the edges of the pile, he located a number
of smaller stones, and picking them up, used them to block
all the holes he could find — all, that is, except the one in
which the wasps had their nest.

When, a short time later, he returned to the vixens, he
found that the stoats were closing in again.

'Is it ready?' asked Vickey.

'As ready as it will ever be,' he told her.

'Right, let's give them a dose of their own medicine.'

Without warning, the three of them charged.   Taken by
surprise, the stoats turned and ran back to the pile of
stones.   There, to their obvious alarm, they found that all
escape routes were blocked, except one, and with the foxes
snapping at their heels they had no option but to take it.
This, of course, was the one with the wasps' nest, and while
in normal circumstances they might have no fear of wasps,
it was another thing to be pushed in on top of them.
Desperately they squirmed around in an effort to get back
out, only to find themselves looking into the fangs of the
foxes.   Turning again, they were forced to run the gauntlet

of the angry wasps who, unlike the foxes, were able to follow them far into the pile of stones.

From the squeals that were coming from below, the foxes could well imagine what was happening. Here and there, they reckoned, the stoats were being cornered, and in cramped spaces, were being forced to fight an enemy that was not only smaller and faster than they were, but carried a nasty sting in its tail!

Vickey smiled, but she wasn't finished yet. 'Now,' she told Little Running Fox, 'go back to the field where you left the three eggs and bring one of them back here.'

'Which one?'

'Any one, it doesn't matter.'

Little Running Fox raced away, and when she returned with one of the eggs, her mother told her to place it near the pile of stones.

'But they wouldn't take it from us before,' she said. 'Why should they take it now?'

'Because their situation has changed,' Vickey explained. 'If your lip is anything to go by, they won't be biting anything solid again for a while, and that includes us.'

'When they find their way out they'll be glad to take the egg,' said Black Tip, 'and then the debt will be paid.'

Little Running Fox smiled. She knew that at long last her nightmare was over.

7: A Time to Dance

BEYOND THE BIRCHES, curlews glided above their breeding grounds in some far corner of the bog, their tremulous call rising and falling in a plaintive yet pleasant song which seemed to emphasise a desire to keep their distance from both man and beast.   On the bog itself, a mass of ferns, no taller than a fox, were springing up, for all the world like a flock of mythical birds rising with curled heads and out-spread wings from the ashes of last summer's fires.   The heather was greening, and it was dotted here and there with white flecks of cottongrass and the occasional yellow head of mouse-eared hawkweed.   The blossoms had now gone from the hawthorn, and the cow parsley was losing its glitter, but the rowan trees and the elder were in full bloom.

Under the birches, Old Sage Brush and the other cubs listened as Little Running Fox told them how she and her parents had finally managed to rid themselves of the stoats. And as she recalled Ratwiddle's advice, the old fox chuckled, saying, 'He's a strange fox all right. A bit scatty, I suppose.'   Turning his head slightly, he joked, 'Sorry Scat, no offence intended.'

The cubs smiled.   They could see the old fox was in good form and was well pleased with the way the stoats had been outwitted.   'Of course,' he added hastily, 'that's not to say poor Ratwiddle hasn't got wisdom.   He has, but then you have to have a certain amount of wisdom to figure it out, and that's no harm I suppose if it makes you think for yourselves.'

The cubs murmured in agreement, and he went on, 'Now,

there's a very important lesson to be learned from this encounter with the stoats, and it's this. You must not be hasty in anything you do. You must think first before you pounce, otherwise you can land yourselves in a lot of trouble.'

They all nodded, and seeing that the moment was right to pass on to something else, Scab stopped scratching and said, 'Sage Brush, you said you might be able to help my itch.'

'Is it still causing you a problem?'

Scab nodded, and realising that the old fox couldn't see him, added, 'It's getting worse.'

'All right, we'll see what we can do to stop it.'

'You said there's a flower on the bog that might help it. Do you think it's the right time of year for it?'

'Every time of the year is the right time of year for something. Now, here's what to look for. . .'

Old Sage Brush directed the cubs to go out and search the bog for a purple flower. Its head hung like a bluebell's, he told them, only it was bigger and taller, and it had a tongue of gold.

The cubs couldn't know it, but they were now looking for a flower which man grandly called *aquilegia vulgaris*, or more commonly, grannybonnets, presumably because of its likeness to a floppy hat which a little old woman might wear. Nor did they know that when man crushed its dried seed, the powder was very effective in killing lice. However, Old Sage Brush knew that in foxlore it was said that the purple flower, if used to line a den, could sometimes help a fox

afflicted with an itch.   He wasn't sure if it would work, but
he thought it was worth a try.

'If it doesn't,' he told the cubs when they had brought the
flower back, 'then we'll have to try and think of something
else.'

It rained during the night, but the young foxes found they
were warm and dry beneath the birches, and Scab now took
comfort from the fact that his den was lined with something
which might ease the dreadful itch which tormented him.

It was midday before the rain stopped.   The skies were
still overcast, and it was very warm.

'It's not great for hunting,' remarked Young Black Tip.

'Well, it depends on what you're looking for,' said Old
Sage Brush.   'How's your mouth Little Running Fox?   Still
sore?'

'The swelling's down a bit, but I don't think I could hunt
yet.'

'If you look around now,' the old fox told her, 'I think you
may find the rain has brought out something you can catch
and eat without too much difficulty.'

Curious, the cubs dashed out to see what it was, and were
delighted to discover that there were numerous black slugs
and snails on the bog.   Twinkle found one slug making its
way up the arching stem of a drooping, bald-headed dande-
lion.   Little Running Fox spotted another on a broad blade
of grass.   Young Black Tip found a snail with a green-striped
cone-shaped shell climbing a dead hogweed stump, while
Scat nosed out a yellow-striped one in among the grass.   For
once Scab forgot his itch and pounced on everything he
could find . . . slugs, snails, and even two white moths which
fluttered up from the heather.

'It won't be long before the frogs emerge from their
breeding pools,' the old fox told them later.   'Then you'll
really have the time of your lives.'

'The pools here on the bog?' asked Twinkle.

The old fox shook his head.   'No, they only use certain
pools and streams.   I'll show you when the time comes.'

'How do you know when it is time for these things?' asked
Scat.

'That is something you must learn.   As I've already told
you, everything has its time, even the frogs.   You will find

that when the adults wake up from their winter sleep, they make their way across the fields to their breeding pools.'

'When is that?' asked Scab.

'Around about our cubbing time. That is why you haven't seen them. Then, on a wet night in the middle of summer, the young frogs which have been born in the pools will decide it is time to leave the water and make their way into the fields.'

'So you get the big ones going to the pools and the small ones coming back?' said Young Black Tip.

Old Sage Brush nodded. 'But now it's time for you to go to the water.'

'What for?' asked Scab, who didn't particularly like the water.

'To learn how to swim, of course.'

Before leaving, the cubs suggested that they should hunt around the edge of the bog for any more food their parents might have left, but the old fox forbade it. Swimming, he told them, was not something to be undertaken on a full stomach. The slugs and snails, of course, had only whetted their appetite, but reluctantly they accepted his word, and off they set for the river on the upper side of the dam. On the way they met Skulking Dog and Sinnéad, and they agreed to go along.

As they approached the river, the cubs galloped on ahead sending several small birds into flight, and causing Old Sage Brush to shake his head.

'That's no way to catch a bird,' he told them. The cubs looked at him, their ears still cocked from the excitement of seeing the birds. 'Most birds have to lift their heads when they're drinking to let the water run down their throats, so they're going to see you, even if you creep up on them.'

'How do we get them then?' asked Young Black Tip.

'You don't,' replied the old fox. 'You keep an eye out for a bird that doesn't lift its head.'

'What bird?' asked Twinkle.

'Well, the wood pigeon doesn't need to lift its head to drink, and its a good deal bigger than the ones you've been chasing. You might remember that for a start.'

Sinnéad and Skulking Dog looked at each other, then at Twinkle and smiled. The old fox might be blind, but they knew he had seen more than most.

Moving up along the bank, they came to a place where the river was spanned by several arches of an old stone bridge, and swallows were skimming the shallow water in search of insects.

'This bridge is the home of starlings, wagtails, kingfishers and dippers,' the old fox informed the cubs. 'Its stones have reared many broods.'

Crouching low among the rushes so as not to be seen, the cubs listened and watched.

'Now,' he went on, 'from the kingfisher you will learn that when you catch a fish you should swallow it head first — otherwise the bones may stick in your throat and choke you. But from the dipper you will learn something else. Look closely at the river and see if you can spot one. It's like a robin, only it's dark brown with a white breast.'

'There's one, over there,' whispered Scab. 'It seems to be dancing on the water — there, just below the bridge.'

The other cubs followed his gaze, and sure enough they saw a small bird standing on a stone that was scarcely above the surface of the water.

'It's bobbing up and down,' observed Little Running Fox. 'And dipping its head in the water.'

'Almost as if it can't wait to go,' added Twinkle.

'Just see where it does go,' said the old fox.

The cubs watched as the dipper darted along almost under the water, and played hide-and-seek around a place where the water gushed over some large stones. Then, to their surprise, it jumped in and walked along the bottom, coming to the surface a short distance farther on.

'What's it doing?' asked Scat.

'It's catching its food under the water,' Old Sage Brush told him, 'and now we're going to try and do the same thing.'

The cubs looked at each other as if to say the old fox had taken leave of his senses. However, Skulking Dog assured them, 'It can be done all right, providing you know how.'

Moving down-river to the lake, they hid among the reeds and long grass and looked out across the water.

'What do you see?' asked the old fox.

'Ducks,' said Scab.

'Some big ones and a clutch of young ones,' added Twinkle.   'They're not far out.'

'Far enough,' remarked the old fox.   'How would you catch one?'

'Wait until it comes in,' suggested Twinkle.

'Ah, but it might not, and then you might starve to death waiting.   No, your father will show you how to do it.'

Quietly, Skulking Dog made his way through the reeds and slipped into the lake.   With his nose just above the water, he swam towards the ducks.   The cubs watched and waited.   The ducks, they could see, were blissfully unaware that he was approaching.   Even so, he went completely under the water.   The cubs held their breath.   Suddenly, one of the ducks disappeared.   One moment it was there, the next it was gone.   Then, just as suddenly, it re-emerged, but this time it was in Skulking Dog's jaws.   With loud quacks of alarm, the other ducks took off, some breaking into flight, those that had young scurrying away from danger as fast as their webbed feet could take them.

Old Sage Brush chuckled.   He knew from the sounds what had happened.   'Well,' he smiled, 'what do you think of that?'

The cubs were too mesmerised to speak.

Emerging from the water, Skulking Dog shook himself and dropped the duck on the grass.   'Now,' he told the cubs, 'it's your turn.'

'Do you think you could do it?' asked Sinnéad.

'If otters and pike can do it,' said the old fox, 'so can they.'

'But we can't swim,' said Young Black Tip.

'Even mink have to learn to swim,' the old fox reminded him.   'And it isn't difficult.   All you have to do is walk in the water, just like the dippers.'

'Like the dippers?' repeated Twinkle.

The old fox nodded.   'More or less.'

It all sounded very simple, but Little Running Fox wasn't convinced.   She looked at the size of the duck and suggested, 'Well, maybe we might be able to catch a young one.'

Old Sage Brush stroked his grey whiskers with his paw and told her, 'You know, I once heard of a fox who lived on a hen's eggs.   And because he ate all the eggs, there were no

chicks.   And because there were no chicks, there were no
other hens.   And then you know what he did?'

The cubs shook their heads and mumbled that they didn't.

'Then he ate the hen, and he had nothing.'   The old fox
curled his tail around until it lay across his nose, and began
to doze.   The cubs were still thinking about what he had
said, and wondering what he meant.

Sinnéad lowered her voice, and explained, 'He means that
if there are no small ducks, there'll be no big ducks, and
they're the ones that provide us with the most food.'

The cubs nodded.   They were beginning to understand.
Or at least they thought they were!

The clouds of the morning had now given way to blue sky
and sunshine.   As Old Sage Brush dozed, the cubs lay
beside him, enjoying the heat of the sun and watching
Twinkle getting her first swimming lessons from Sinnéad
and Skulking Dog.

'It really is like walking in water,' Sinnéad was assuring
her.

The others smiled, and Young Black Tip said, 'I never
thought we would be able to hunt in the lake.'

Hearing him, the old fox lifted his head.   'You must learn
to use the water for many things — to catch fish, hunt birds,
and perhaps more important, to help you escape from man
and his dogs.'

'Is Sinnéad really your daughter?' asked Little Running
Fox.

The old fox nodded.

'And did Skulking Dog really rescue her from the howling
dogs?'

Once again the old fox nodded, and Scab said, 'He's a
strong fox, isn't he?'

'One of the strongest,' agreed the old fox.   'But it was his
cunning that outwitted the howling dogs, not his strength.'

The cubs found that learning to swim was great fun, and
they played around at the water's edge until at last Old Sage
Brush told them it was time to go.   'It's dangerous to stay in
one place too long,' he warned.   'Other eyes may be
watching us, and I have no way of seeing them.'

On the way back to the bog, they parted company with
Skulking Dog and Sinnéad who were returning to Beech

Paw, and continued on up the hill.

'Does man really wear a coat the colour of spindle berries when he hunts us?' asked Little Running Fox.

'He does when he hunts us with the howling dogs,' replied the old fox.

'And what colour is that?' asked Scab.

The old fox stopped.   'It's a peculiar sort of red.'

'You mean, like the sky at night, when it glows above the hills?' said Twinkle.

'Not really.   It's very difficult to describe.   It's like . . .'

'Like the colour of blood,' suggested Young Black Tip rather coldly.

The other cubs shivered and looked at him.

'Maybe,' said the old fox.   'It's so long since I've seen it, I can't exactly recall.   But when you hear the howling dogs coming, don't hang around to find out.   Just run for your life.'

'What should we do if we are hunted by the howling dogs?' asked Scab.

'The hedges will be bare, and the spindle berries up at the blackthorns will be bright.   But if you think you cannot make it to Beech Paw, make for the river.'

'And if we can't do that?' asked Young Black Tip.

'Then make for the nearest evergreens.   The smell of pine is strong, too strong for the howling dogs.   It will smother your scent and confuse them.   But there are many tricks, and you will need them all.'

They moved on and were still talking about the howling dogs when Hop-along and his mate came running down a hedgerow towards them. Scab and Scat immediately bounded forward to meet them, but were turned back with a warning that there was danger up ahead.

'What is it?' asked Old Sage Brush.

'Man and his fun dogs,' Hop-along informed him. 'They're in a hollow, just over the hill.'

'Are they following you?'

'No,' said She-la.   'They were too busy digging to notice us.'

'Digging?   Digging for what?'

'I dont' know,' said She-la.   'Perhaps another fox.'

The cubs were alert now, wondering what was happening and ready to run.

Old Sage Brush considered the situation for a moment.
'Can you see them without getting too close?'

'We saw them from the top of the hill,' Hop-along told him.
'They didn't see us, but we were afraid you might walk into
them.'

'And we very well might have — thanks.'

'You must return to the bog by another path,' urged She-
la.

Old Sage Brush agreed, but yet he made no move to go.
Hop-along looked at She-la and knew she was thinking the
same thing.   Once, a long time ago, man and his fun dogs
had dug the old fox and his family out of their earth. Only
Sinnéad and himself had survived, and he had been
blinded.

'If it's a fox, maybe there's something we can do,' he said.

Knowing the high degree of danger that awaited them
over the hill, neither Hop-along nor She-la offered him any
word of encouragement.

'Do you think we could have a closer look?' he asked
them.

'It's very risky,' replied Hop-along.

'Maybe if you didn't stay too long,' said She-la.

'All right.   Let's just have a quick look, and then we'll be
off.   Young Black Tip, go up and see if the way is clear.'

The cub raced off up the fields and returned a short time
later to tell him that man and his dogs were all occupied
with the dig.

'And the wind?'

'It's in our favour.'

'Good,' said the old fox.   'Now be quiet, every one of
you, and if you have to run, run for the river.   With luck the
water will wash away your scent.'

As they neared the top of the hill, the wind brought
noises to the ears of Old Sage Brush that were familiar and
disturbing ... the noises of men shouting and small dogs
barking.   Hop-along and She-la had heard them before too,
but it was a new experience for the cubs.

Taking great care, they crept forward until they were at a
hedge overlooking the hollow.   For a moment nothing was
said, and the old fox knew that the others were now seeing
the last thing he had seen before he was blinded — man and

his fun dogs digging out an earth.

The cubs looked at the scene, eyes wide, ears erect and twitching at every sound. They were frightened and shocked by what they saw, and hung back, ready to go.

'Settle down,' whispered the old fox. 'They're too busy with what they're doing to notice us. Now Scab, tell me what you see.'

Scab shuffled forward on his belly to get a better view.

The earth was in a steep bank under a hedge, he told him. Some men were gathered around the entrance, and there were more in the higher field on the opposite side of the hedge. Several others, with small fun dogs straining and whining at the leash, were standing back, waiting.

'What exactly are they doing?' asked Old Sage Brush.

'The men at the entrance seem to be listening,' Scab told him.

'That means they've sent in a small dog to find out where the foxes are,' explained the old fox. 'When they hear it barking inside, they'll know the earth is occupied.'

'Then what?' asked Twinkle.

'Then the men up in the other field will try and find out where exactly the foxes are. When they do, they'll dig down.'

'They're doing something now,' said Little Running Fox.

Scab eased himself up to see. 'They're making holes in the ground with long iron bars.'

The old fox sighed. 'The jabbing poles. That's what blinded me'

The cubs looked at him in a way that showed they were sorry for the tragedy that had befallen him, but admired the fact that he had survived it.

Having made a number of holes with the iron bars, and listened intently to the sounds below, the men in the upper field discarded their coats, and taking up picks and shovels, began to dig. Behind them, terriers danced on their hind legs and struggled to get free.

'Why don't the foxes make a run for it?' wondered Scat.

'Because they've blocked all the holes except one,' Old Sage Brush told him, 'and there's a dog in that one.

Down at the entrance, a man wearing a greasy cap got up from his knees, and the foxes watched as he walked back and sat down beside a small, black mongrel that was tied to the base of a hawthorn bush. The dog's face was badly scarred and its eyes were bulging as it strained on the leash. The man said something to it and lit his pipe.

'That's the trapper,' Hop-along informed the cubs.

A large grey dog trotted over to the man, and he put his arm around it and patted it on the ribs. Unlike the terriers, it didn't seem very interested in what was going on.

'That dog isn't on a leash,' warned She-la.

'What's it like?' asked Old Sage Brush.

'It's a funny sort of dog,' observed Scab. 'It has hardly any tail.'

'But it has strong legs and powerful jaws,' noted Hop-along.

'Which means it's fast and has a good nose,' said the old fox.

With a blind fox on one side of her, a lame fox on the other, and a dog on the loose, She-la thought it was time they should be going.

'In a minute,' said the old fox. However, time passed and still he made no move to go. He was listening to every sound from the hollow, and when there were shouts of excitement from the men in the upper field, he asked, 'What are they doing now?'

'I think they've dug down to the earth,' Scab told him. 'They're very excited.'

'They're all gathered around,' said She-la, 'and I think they must have put in more dogs. The other dogs are going mad to get in too.'

The men continued to dig. They were sweating and swearing as they worked in relays to enlarge the hole. All around them dogs and their owners were craning their necks to see what was going on, and excitement was at fever pitch.

Suddenly, most of the onlookers took a step back, and Scab told Old Sage Brush that someone had pulled the trapper's little black dog out of the earth by its hind legs. It in turn seemed to be pulling something else.

The trapper himself was now holding an iron bar in each hand. One had a heart-shaped handle, the other a curved handle like a walking stick. Putting them down into the hole handles first, he threaded one through the other and squeezed them together. When, a moment later, he pulled them out, the cubs could see they had been put into a vice-like grip across the neck of a badger. Furthermore, the dog was still holding on to the badger's face.

'And there's blood all over them,' exclaimed Little Running Fox.

With the help of someone else, the trapper persuaded his dog to release its grip. Then, handing the iron bars to another man, he reached down, caught the badger by its short yellowish tail, and held it up. The badger continued to struggle and tried to get its head up around to bite him, but because of its stocky build it was unable to get near him. A small metal cage was opened, and with the help of other men using spades, the trapper manoeuvred the badger into it.

'Have they got it?' asked Old Sage Brush.

The trapper had now secured the door of the cage, and straightening up, took out his pipe once more, apparently well satisfied with his work.

'I'm afraid so,' said She-la.   'They have it in a cage.'

'And what's that the trapper has around his neck?' asked Scat.   'It looks like a rabbit's paw.'

She-la focussed her eyes on the paw that adorned the trapper's neck, but didn't reply. All the cubs were staring at it now too.

Hop-along limped forward to get a better look at it.   Then his eyes opened wide, and he exclaimed, 'That's not a rabbit's paw.   That's my paw!'

8: A Time to Speak

REALISING THAT the men and their dogs would soon depart from the hollow and go their separate ways, Old Sage Brush finally decided it was time to leave.

'Where will you go?' asked She-la. 'They're between you and the bog, so you can't go back there.'

'We'll have to split up,' replied the old fox. 'There are too many of us, and we can't run the risk of the fun dogs coming across our scent, especially the big one with the stumpy tail.' He considered the situation for a moment. 'I tell you what She-la. You go back to Beech Paw. Tell the others what has happened, and warn them to be on the alert. Hop-along, you know if you go farther up the river there's a small glen?'

'The one with the old mill?' said Hop-along. 'But that's not in our territory.'

'Never mind. Take Scab and Scat and make your way across country to it. I'll go back down to the river with the others and we'll get to it from there. Hurry. The small dogs may be tired, but the big one isn't.'

The place where the cubs were now being taken was a small wooded valley that nestled in the middle of an area of rich farmland. It had been long regarded by farmers as too steep to cultivate. However, it had been cultivated in another way by the people who had bought it. They had allowed it to become a sort of wildlife sanctuary, a place where birds and animals could live and breed, free from the pressures of man.

A stream trickled into the valley, widened into a muddy

pond and tumbled down a course that had once driven a large mill wheel. The wheel was still, only a splintered skeleton of what it used to be, but the ruined mill and its waterways, which had given life to man in the form of flour, now sustained a variety of wildlife. Dippers scudded across the shallow waterfalls, while the pond was the home of ducks, water-hens, coots and herons.

On the sides of the valley grew tall oak trees, beeches, birches, sycamore, chestnut and Scots pine, and in the swaying tops of many of them colonies of rooks had built their nests. While in the surrounding fields, spring would produce crops which were almost free of weeds, the valley would provide a more colourful growth — wild flowers such as marsh marigolds, bluebells, primroses, forget-me-nots, wood anemonies, and dog violets, as well as a variety of butterflies, like the common blue and hedge brown.

Small birds abounded in the undergrowth, and below them lived badgers, foxes, rabbits and many other forms of life. Small though the valley was, there was a place for them all . . . even Old Sage Brush and his fellow foxes now that they had nowhere else to go.

Hop-along was first to arrive, and as he waited for the others, he lay in the undergrowth and talked to his cubs.

'Well Scab,' he said, with an affectionate rub of his nose, 'how have you been keeping? How's the itch? Is it any better?'

'A bit.' Scab scratched now that he thought about it. 'At least I think it is.'

'Old Sage Brush has given him something to line his den with,' said Scat. 'It's a flower we got on the bog.'

'Well, if anyone knows what'll help it, it's him.'

'But it's still sore,' said Scab.

'I know,' said Hop-along. 'I know. But give it a try and with a bit of luck you'll be all right. The old fox knows what he's doing.'

'Anyway, how are you?' asked Scat. 'How are you managing?'

Hop-along smiled. 'I'm fine. So's your mother, but I think she misses you up around the blackthorns. You know what vixens are like.'

The cubs nodded, in a grown-up sort of way, but Hop-along could see the feeling was mutual, and was pleased to think that they probably missed the blackthorns too.

Fortunately, Old Sage Brush and the other cubs arrived just then, and all thoughts of the blackthorns were forgotten. The old fox immediately went into a nearby earth to make contact with the local foxes and when he came out he announced that they could stay until the danger passed.

'Do you think there's any danger of pursuit?' asked Hop-along.

The old fox shook his head. 'I don't think so. Man and his dogs have found what they were looking for. Anyway they are not welcome here.'

They were all lying together now in deep cover on the side of the valley.

'I remember once, when I could see,' the old fox told the cubs, 'there was a large yew tree in front of one of the houses.'

'It's still there,' said Scab.

'I saw five different kinds of birds nesting in it at the same time. Some were so small they collected cobwebs to make their nests, and some of the nests were so low man could reach up and touch them, but he never did.'

'But do the creatures here not live off each other the way they do everywhere else?' asked Little Running Fox.

'Of course they do, but only to the extent that they need to.'

Scab sat back and scratched himself vigorously. 'Then why can't we stay here?'

'Because, as your father has said, this is the territory of other foxes. If we stayed, it would upset the balance.'

'What balance?' asked Scat.

'The balance of nature.' The old fox cocked an ear to the evening breeze and listened to the sounds of the small birds singing. 'You see, in this glen, nature is in harmony. The green caterpillars feed on the leaves. The blue tits feed on the caterpillars. The hawks feed on the blue tits. And the foxes feed on anything they can. That is the way nature has arranged it. But too many of anything — or too few of them — could upset that arrangement.'

He sighed and went on, 'Here man seems to understand.

He knows everything has its use.   But elsewhere, out there in the fields, he does not.   He has no time for the birds, no room for the trees.   He dredges the rivers and drains the meadows.   He takes away the hedges to make the fields bigger, and then burns the stubble when he has harvested the corn.'

'He has no time for anything he feels is no use to him,' said Hop-along.

The old fox grunted.   'Even when they are of use to him, it makes no difference.   The birds eat the grubs, and he begrudges them grain.   We kill the rats, and he denies us a hen.'

'Yet he seems to think he has the right to come and steal the coats off our backs,' said Hop-along.

'Is that really why he hunts us?' asked Twinkle.   'So that he can take our coats for himself?'

Hop-along nodded.   'We saw it for ourselves on our journey to man's place.   It takes many of our coats to make one for him.   Little wonder we've almost been hunted out of existence.'

'Almost, but not quite,' said the old fox.   'There are still some of us left, and we've fine healthy cubs to make sure that we will be around for a long time.'

The cubs smiled, and Little Running Fox asked, 'I wonder why man hunts the badger?'

'I don't know,' confessed the old fox, 'but you can be sure it's for no good purpose.'

'You might as well ask why does man hang my paw around his neck,' said Hop-along.   'He does many things we cannot understand.'

'How can you be sure it was your paw we saw?' asked Young Black Tip.

'Because I've known the trapper a long time — and I've known my paw even longer.'

'Very few foxes have the courage to chew off their own paw to escape from man,' said the old fox.   'So I doubt if it belongs to anyone else.'

Twinkle was still thinking of the scenes in the hollow.   'I wonder if man can talk?'

Old Sage Brush sniffed the breeze for any hint of pursuit, and remarked, 'Well, he makes enough noise, doesn't he?'

'But I thought animals were the only ones that could talk,' said Little Running Fox.

The old fox shrugged.   'If we can talk, why can't man?' He chuckled and added, 'Then, of course, maybe man thinks *he* is the only one who can talk.'

The cubs laughed at the idea, and Scat asked, 'How could he think that?'

'How indeed,' said the old fox.   'But the way he acts you would think he thinks we can't even think.   You know, that we have a mind of our own, a right to exist.'

The cubs thought about that for a moment.

'But he knows we are cunning, doesn't he?' asked Young Black Tip.   'You said so.'   When the old fox nodded, he added, 'Then he must know we can think.'

'And he must have heard the sounds we make,' said Little Running Fox.   'So he must know we can talk.'

'Unless he doesn't understand what we are saying,' suggested Twinkle.

'We don't understand the language of the birds,' said Old Sage Brush, 'but we know they can talk.'

'True,' reflected Hop-along.   'We know that they sing for a mate, and warn other birds that they're not welcome.'

'And a blackbird warns everybody,' said Scat.

Hop-along smiled.   'That's right.   Even a rabbit can warn of danger, and it's not very bright.'

Scab stopped scratching to ask, 'How?'

'It thumps the ground with a hind paw.'

'All man has to do to know we can talk is look at his own dog,' Old Sage Brush went on.   'When he is out hunting it tells him with its tail what it sees with its nose.   It wags its tail when it's happy, puts it between its legs when it's afraid. It barks at strangers, howls at foxes.'

'It even howls at the wide eye of gloomglow,' said Hop-along.

The cubs were amused, and the old fox told them, 'Apart from our voices, man should know we also talk with our scents and our marks — something, I believe, he cannot do. Fortunately he cannot read as well as we can either, otherwise he would learn much from the messages we leave — things about our territory, our sex, our condition, even whether we are young or old — and we wouldn't want him to know things like that, would we?'

The cubs shook their heads and agreed wholeheartedly.

'But surely there are many things that must tell him he's not the only one can talk,' said Hop-along.

'Like what?' asked Scat.

'Well, like the cuckoo.   Doesn't he hear it telling him that summer has come?   Doesn't he see the wild geese following their leader across the sky and hear them calling out that winter is on the way?   Doesn't his own hen sing to tell him she is going to lay?   Doesn't his cow remind him that she has to be milked?   Doesn't his rooster let him know it is time to get up and attend to all of these things?'

'All things can talk,' agreed the old fox, 'and man should know that.   Even the flowers can talk to the bees, and the bees can talk to each other.'

Young Black Tip was about to ask how the bees and flowers could talk, when something came bundling down through the undergrowth and almost crashed in on top of them. Startled, they were already making a run for it, when they realised that it was a badger and two of her cubs.

Seeing that they were distressed, Hop-along paused and asked, 'Are you being chased?'

The sow badger had to wait for a moment to get her breath.   'No,' she replied.   'But they tried to dig us out.'

Old Sage Brush came back to her and inquired, 'Over in the hollow?'

'That's right.   How did you know?'

'We saw them digging,' Hop-along told her.   'How did you get away?'

The badger cubs were fairly big, but not fully weaned, and they leaned against their mother, frightened and shivering. 'My mate held back the dogs while we dug deeper.   He put up a great fight.'

'He did put up a great fight,' Hop-along assured her.   'We saw it all.   But they got him in the end.   The trapper has him.'

The badger sank to the ground.   'I was afraid of that. We couldn't find him anywhere.'

'What will they do with him?' asked Little Running Fox.

'What they always do,' said the badger, 'torment him with their dogs.'

'But that's horrible,' said Twinkle.

'Will he be all right?' asked Scat.

The badger sighed. 'It all depends. If they don't break his jaw, he may have a chance.'

'Break his jaw?' exclaimed Twinkle. 'Why should they do that?'

'If they're training their dogs and don't want them hurt, that's what they do,' said the badger. 'But if they're trying to see which dog is best, they may not.'

'Maybe he'll be able to fight them off,' suggested Young Black Tip. 'He seemed to be very strong.'

'He is now,' replied the badger. 'But he won't be able to eat their food, and if they keep him too long he'll get weak. Then, if they're trying to see which of their dogs is the best, it'll be hard on him for they'll be the toughest dogs they have.'

'I wish there was something we could do,' said Twinkle.

The badger shook her striped head. 'There's nothing any of us can do now.'

'Maybe we could open the cage and let him out,' suggested Scab.

'We tried that before,' the badger told him, 'when one of our friends was caught, but we couldn't do it.'

'Where will this take place?' asked Old Sage Brush. 'This match between your mate and the fun dogs.'

'There's a pit not far from here. Once they put him into it he won't be able to get out.'

'Could you show us where it is?'

'You mean, all of you?'

'No. Just one or two.'

'If you think it would do any good!'

'It can't do any harm.'

'All right,' said the badger. 'Just as soon as we get settled into a new set.'

'Maybe they'll let you stay here for a while,' suggested the old fox. 'Anyway, wherever you are, leave a message for us at the edge of the bog, say at the nearest point to the birches. We'll find it.'

Dusk was almost upon them, and knowing that it was now safe to leave, Old Sage Brush decided it was time they were on their way. They made their way down the stream and

around the edge of the pond to the old mill.   There the old
fox and Scab concealed themselves in a clump of brambles
beside a waterfall and waited while the others rooted
around for something to eat.

'I thought you said we couldn't hunt here,' whispered
Scab.

'I didn't say that,' answered the old fox, 'I said we couldn't
stay.   But it would be a shame to leave without getting
something — there's so much of it, isn't there?'

Scab watched the foam bubbling and frothing here and
there below the waterfall.   Twinkle was poking her nose
into it, sniffing for ducks or anything else she could find, and
as she came back up to them he asked, 'Well, any luck?'

'Not yet,' she replied, 'but there's plenty of food around.
I can smell it.'

Scab sniggered.

'What are you laughing at?' she asked indignantly.

'Your mouth.   It's all froth.'

Old Sage Brush smiled. 'You want to be careful
Twinkle.'

'Why?'

'Because, with froth on your mouth man might think
you're a mad dog.'

Twinkle shook her head to flick the froth away, stuck her
nose in the air and resumed her search.   Sensing by her
silence that she had ignored him, Old Sage Brush chuckled
with amusement.   Scab laughed and continued to scratch.

That night, Hop-along returned to the blackthorns, while
Old Sage Brush and the cubs went back to the bog where
they curled up in the comfort and security of the birches.

Twinkle listened to the familiar rustle of the wind in the
leaves, but her thoughts were elsewhere.   'Do you think we
might be able to help the badgers?' she asked the old fox.

'Perhaps.'

'Why should we help them?' asked Young Black Tip.

'Because we owe it to them, that's why,' said the old fox.
'You see, shortly after you were born we asked them to help
us destroy the dam man was building at the far end of the
lake.'

'And did they?' asked Twinkle.

'They did, and so did a lot of other animals who live in the valley.   But we couldn't do it.'

'I didn't know that,' said Young Black Tip.

Old Sage Brush smiled.   'How could you?   But apart from that, many of our earths have been dug by badgers. They are great diggers and if man kills them we will have to dig for ourselves.'   He rested his head on his legs and added, 'Now that's something you might all sleep on.'

Two evenings later, the badger took Young Black Tip, Twinkle and Scat across the fields to show them where man's fun dogs would be fighting her mate.

Following a small stream which trickled along the bottom of a ditch, she led them to a place where a farmer had constructed a drinking place for his cattle.   This consisted of a concrete base enclosed by three low walls.   The base sloped down to the stream to give the cattle a firm footing, and the walls had been built at the sides and back, leaving the front open so that the cattle could come and go as they pleased.   Pipes had been laid along the bottom of the ditch on either side of the enclosure, so that the water would flow freely through it.

As the three cubs looked at it and tried to understand what it was for, Young Black Tip asked, 'Was it built for badgers?'

'No,' the badger told them.   'It's for cattle when they want to drink.   But the trapper and his friends will build a wall across the front and make it into a pit.'

'What about the water?' asked Twinkle.

'They build a small dam across the stream, farther back along the ditch, before it enters the pipe.'

'Then what's to stop your mate escaping through the pipes?' asked Scat.

'Inside the pit, they put stones against the pipes and there's no way he can get out.   Anyway, if he went into the pipes they'd only send the dogs in after him, and if he couldn't turn he wouldn't have a chance.   They'd tear him to pieces.'

The cubs shuddered at the very thought of that, and hurried back to the birches to report to Old Sage Brush.

'Describe it to me,' said the old fox, 'so that I may see it in my mind's eye.'

Between them, the three cubs told him what they had seen, and when they described how the water was piped in one side and out the other, he asked, just as Scat had done, 'Why can't the badger get out that way too?'

Scat told him how man blocked each pipe in the pit with a large stone, and added, 'Anyway, if the boar is much bigger than his mate he would be a tight fit.'

'The pipe where the water flows in is longer, but it's wider than the other one,' said Twinkle. 'He might be able to make it through that. But as Scat says, it's blocked.'

'Where do the pipes begin and end?'

'They both run along the bottom of the ditch for a short distance,' explained Young Black Tip, 'and then they just open out into the stream.'

Old Sage Brush lifted his head and asked them, 'Well, what do you think?'

'If one of us went down the big pipe, maybe we could help push out the stone from the inside,' suggested Twinkle.

'But you said the big pipe was longer. What if man came along and saw that the stone had been moved? He would know you were inside and put his small dogs in after you. Then you would be in trouble as well as the badger.'

'Still,' said Scat. 'We'd like to help them.'

'I know you would,' said the old fox. 'But if you are not to end up in the pit yourselves you will require a better plan than that.'

The cubs knew Old Sage Brush was right, and that night they thought and thought about it, and wondered what they could do. By morning, the semblance of a plan had formed in their minds, but when they outlined it to the old fox, he shook his head, saying, 'No, it's too dangerous. I couldn't let you risk it.'

'But it would only take two of us,' said Twinkle, 'and it could work.'

'Which two?'

'It would have to be Twinkle and me,' said Scat. 'We're the smallest.'

'No, it might not work. I couldn't allow it.'

'Please,' implored Twinkle. 'At least let us try.'

Old Sage Brush nodded his head slowly as he weighed up the possibilities. 'I tell you what,' he said at last, 'when gloomglow comes we'll ask your parents and see what they think.'

That seemed to satisfy the cubs, and during the night, having left Young Black Tip in charge, Old Sage Brush followed Scab through the darkened fields to Beech Paw.

Man had long since left the countryside to the creatures of the night, and the beeches seemed to whisper sweetly in glorious isolation as the adult foxes gathered in a circle beneath them and talked by the light of the moon.

Hop-along and She-la were delighted to see Scab again, and curious to know what his brother Scat was up to.

'He wants to help the badgers.' Old Sage Brush informed them. 'They all do.'

'How?' asked Hop-along.

Briefly the old fox outlined the badgers' predicament, and the plan the cubs had come up with.

'So what it all comes down to,' said Black Tip, 'is that if Scat can make man think the badger has squeezed into the small pipe, it will give Twinkle time to help it escape through the larger one?'

'That about sums it up,' said the old fox. There was silence, and he asked, 'Well, what do you think?'

She-la looked at her mate, Hop-along, and then at Old Sage Brush.   'So Scat would have to go into the small pipe?'

The old fox nodded.

'And is he sure he would get out in time?' asked Hop-along.

'He says the small pipe is shorter, and given half a chance he can do it.'

'And Twinkle would be in the larger one?' said Skulking Dog.

'That's right.   Her and the badger.'

'What if it doesn't work, and the small dogs go in after them?' asked Sinnéad.

'That's the risk they'll be taking.   That's why I wanted it to be your decision.'

'And what about the trapper's other dog?' asked Hop-along.   'The big one with the stumpy tail?'

'Young Black Tip thinks he can keep it occupied, and I've told him a trick or two that should help.'

Vickey sat up with a start and gave her mate an anxious

look. Until now she hadn't realised that one of her cubs would be involved.

'Do you think they can do it?' asked Black Tip.

'They seem to think so.'

'And what do you think?' asked Skulking Dog.

'I think they could pull it off — with a little luck.'

The vixens were silent.

'Well Sinnéad?' asked the old fox.

Sinnéad was obviously very concerned for the safety of the cubs, especially Twinkle, as she was the only one of her litter that had survived. At the same time, she had great faith in her father, so she told him, 'If you say they can do it, I suppose it's all right with us.'

'She-la?'

She-la also had very mixed feelings about it. Scab and Scat were all she and Hop-along had left, and she knew that with the itch Scab had, his chances of survivial weren't good. She didn't want to put Scat at unnecessary risk, but then she knew he must take risks sooner or later. So she just said, 'All right. But may Vulpes be with them.'

When the others had returned to their earths, Old Sage Brush had a quiet word with Black Tip and Vickey.

'What do you think Vickey?' he asked. 'You were my inspiration on our great journey before the cubs were born. Am I right, or am I putting the cubs in unnecessary danger?'

Vickey smiled and recalled, 'It was in this very circle of beeches that we met and decided to seek the secret of survival. You showed us how to be cunning again, and now that the cubs are also learning to be cunning, I suppose we cannot deny them the opportunity.'

Black Tip agreed, and Old Sage Brush nodded, saying, 'That's what I was thinking, but it's nice to hear you say so too.'

9: A Time to Get

THE MEADOW GRASS was now as tall as the unripe barley, and its seed heads had taken on a purple blush as they bowed and swayed beneath the summer breeze. The haws had begun to redden, and the climbing dog rose was in flower, its new leaves as fine as the finest vetch. Up in the blackthorns, small green plums were forming, and there was a sprinkling of tiny flowers on the spindle trees. Deep in the hedgerows, young birds were spreading their wings, while in other nests, visible only in the morning dew, small spiders scrambled around under cobweb covers, waiting for the day when they would spin their own threads and float away on the wind.

Beneath the birches on the bog, the fox cubs also lay and waited. They had expected to hear from the sow badger before now, but she hadn't come and they wondered what had happened. Twinkle jumped as several seed pods on a nearby gorse bush burst in the heat and showered her with seed.

'Are you nervous?' asked Young Black Tip.

Twinkle smiled. 'A little, I suppose.'

'It's all this waiting,' said Scat. 'It gives you time to think.'

'You know, about the small fun dogs and what would happen if they caught us in the pipes,' Twinkle told him.

'But they won't,' Young Black Tip assured her. 'Haven't we gone over it all with Old Sage Brush?'

'Still,' said Twinkle, 'you know what it's like when you start thinking about it.'

'And it's almost a week now,' said Scat. 'I wonder why we haven't heard from her?'

The others shook their heads and were silent.

After a while Little Running Fox got up, saying, 'I think it's time we found out what's going on.'

'So do I,' said Young Black Tip. 'She should have been in touch with us by now.'

Old Sage Brush, who had been listening to what they were saying, was nodding his head, and without further discussion, Young Black Tip and his sister slipped away. At the edge of the bog they split up and searched around, but there was still no message from the badger. Nor could they find any trace of her in the general area, so they decided to go to the glen in case she was still there. However, as they made their way up through the fields, they met another fox. He wasn't much older than they were, and was obviously very agitated. Glancing back over his shoulder, he warned them, 'The trapper's dog. It's on the loose.'

'Which one?' asked Young Black Tip.

'The big grey one. The one with the stumpy tail. It's galloping all over the place.'

'Any sign of the trapper?' inquired Little Running Fox.

The other fox was looking back over his shoulder again, anxious to be on his way. 'Back there, in the corner of a field. There are a lot of men, and they have all their fun dogs — you know, the little wicked ones.'

'Do they have a badger in a cage?' asked Young Black Tip. 'We saw them digging one out in the hollow.'

'I don't know. I didn't wait around long enough to find out — and I don't think you should either.'

With that, he bounded away along the hedgerow.

'What do you think?' asked Little Running Fox. 'Do you think it's the badger fight?'

'It must be.'

'I wonder why the sow badger didn't come and tell us?'

'How could she, with the trapper's big dog on the loose?'

'I hope we're not too late.'

'So do I,' said Young Black Tip. 'Quickly, you go back to the bog and alert Scat and Twinkle.'

'And what about you? Where are you going?'

'I'll go on ahead. Tell the others to join me as soon as they can, and warn them to be on the look-out for the big dog.'

'All right,' said Little Running Fox, 'but you be careful, won't you?'

Young Black Tip promised her he would, and realising there was no more time for talk, they sped off in different directions.

By retracing the scent of the fox they had just met, Young Black Tip located the field where the men were gathered, and even from the safe distance of a bracken-covered hillside, recognized it as the one containing the badger pit.

Knowing well that what they were doing was illegal, the men had chosen the cattle's drinking place for the pit, because it was in a secluded corner of a low-lying field well away from the public roads.

In his hiding place on the hillside, Young Black Tip lay and watched. The wind was blowing towards him, and his large black ears twitched as he listened to the shouts and yelps of excitement. He couldn't see the badger, but he knew it was in the pit. The big dog, he noted, had now returned to the trapper. It had apparently got tired of nosing around on its own and had been drawn back by the yelping of the other dogs. At least, he thought, that was something to be grateful for.

A short time later, Twinkle and Scat slipped in beside him.

'Well,' asked Scat, 'what do you think?'

Young Black Tip's eyes were still riveted on the activity around the badger pit. 'We can't do anything for the moment,' he told them. 'They're too close to it.'

'So is the big dog,' observed Twinkle. 'Do you think you'll be able to keep it occupied long enough for us to get in and out?'

'I hope so.'

'I hope so too,' said Scat. 'Otherwise the trapper will have a few more paws to hang around his neck.'

Realising the implications of that remark, they all looked at each other, but said nothing.

The sun was beating down on the hillside and the wind continued to carry the sounds of man's amusement to the watching fox cubs. Now and then the big dog with the stumpy tail wandered away again, almost as if it was tiring of man's game. Each time the cubs got to their feet, ready to run.   Each time, however, they could see it being drawn back by the sounds behind it, as, one by one, the terriers were dropped into the badger, and the men crowded around the walls of the pit to urge them on.

As far as the foxes were concerned, what was happening was just another instance of man's cruelty.   They had no way of knowing this was only the first step in a process that was as cruel to the dogs as it was to the badgers.   For the object was to train the terriers and test them for badger-baiting competitions later on.   Only the best dogs would be considered good enough for those, and even they would not emerge unscathed.

During the morning, a number of terriers had been dropped in to face the captive badger, and although stiff from his long confinement in the small wire cage, and weak from not being able to feed on his usual diet of worms and beetles, he was putting up a very spirited fight.

Several terriers had faced up to him with great courage. Some had found their mark, so that his face, ears and hind-quarters were now smeared with blood.   However, he also had found his mark, causing severe injuries.

Those terriers that were mauled were lifted out and laid on the ground.   Even in their agony they looked up at their masters with the same loyalty that had driven them to face the badger.   It was as if they were saying they had done their best.   But for one or two of them, their best was not good enough.   Their loyalty would be rewarded by death, for what use was a dog with only one eye or a mangled leg?

Now as the fox cubs watched, there was another flurry of excitement.   A small brown and white terrier had slipped and found its throat in the vice-like grip of the badger's jaws.   The trapper hurriedly caught the badger around the neck with long-handled tongs, while another man prized his jaws open with a crowbar.   The terrier fell free, but its eyes were closed, its body limp, and everyone knew its badger-baiting days were over.

As the body was removed from the pit, the trapper's little black dog and several others which had survived without serious injury, quivered and strained at their leash in a crazed effort to get back in.   The blood on their bodies was mostly the badger's, but the crimson stains were nothing to

the blood lust in their bulging eyes.

For those that lay whimpering and dying, however, the fight was over, and their owners, not wishing to lose any more dogs, were now proposing that the badger's jaw be broken.   This led to a heated argument, and it continued as all concerned picked up their dogs and retreated to another corner of the field where they could wash away the blood and dirt, assess the extent of the injuries, and decide what to do.

The cubs, of course, were unaware that the fate of the badger was now in the balance.   All they could see was that for some reason or other, the men had taken a break.

'Now's our chance,' said Scat.

'Wait,' whispered Twinkle. 'Look. The big dog. It's gone back.'

While the men argued and tended their terriers, the trapper's big dog had returned to sniff around the badger pit.

'I'll try and draw it off,' said Young Black Tip.

Before the others could say anything, he was gone, and they watched as he circled around until he was away up in the fields on the far side of the pit.   They knew the wind was now blowing his scent down towards the big dog. Anxiously, they held their breath and waited to see what would happen.

The big dog lifted its head and sniffed the breeze.

'Look, it's got wind of him,' said Twinkle.

Without so much as a bark, the big dog turned and galloped away towards the place where Young Black Tip had stopped.

'Come on,' said Scat.   'Now's our chance.'

Rising from their hiding place in the bracken, Scat and Twinkle raced down along the hedgerows.   About a field's length from the badger pit, they separated and hopping down into the ditches, kept going until they came to the pipes.

As soon as Young Black Tip saw that the big dog was coming towards him, he took off as fast as his legs could carry him.   He knew that if it got too close to him he wouldn't stand a chance.   However, he was well ahead of it and was now moving down-wind.   Pausing only long enough to make sure that it was on his trail, he kept going in a wide circle. Then, having completed the circle, he continued until he had done half of it again. The dog, he could see, was still on his trail, but he was well down-wind of it. Crouching down, he used all the strength he could muster to jump clear of the scent path he had made. A quick glance to make sure he hadn't been spotted, and he raced back to the hillside where he concealed himself in the bracken again.

Making the circle and then jumping clear of it was an idea he had got from Old Sage Brush, and as he lay panting in the bracken, he hoped it would work. Anxiously he watched as the big dog galloped down along his scent path. It was moving with a strength and apparent ease which he found frightening. At the spot where he had jumped out of the circle it stopped and sniffed the air. Old Sage Brush was right, he thought, it had a good nose. Could it possibly have detected the point where he had jumped off and the scent had weakened? Perhaps, but it wasn't sure. A moment of indecision, and then it was on its way again.

Young Black Tip smiled. With a bit of luck it would continue to run around in circles until the others had done their work. He looked down towards the badger pit. There was no sign of them, and he wondered how they were getting on.

Because Scat was in the shorter pipe, he reached the badger first. He encountered only a dribble of water, but he smelled blood in it and could imagine the dreadful snapping, tearing and biting that had been going on. Shuffling up to the stone which the men had put in the pit to block the pipe, he stopped and listened. All he could hear was the heavy breathing of the wounded boar, and it was only now, as he was about to speak to him, that he realised he didn't know his name. The sow badger hadn't told them. And so, squeezing his nose up over the top of the stone, he just whispered as loudly as he dared, that he had come to help.

A combination of hunger, fright and pain had left the badger in a state of shock. He no longer knew where he was or what he was doing. He wasn't even aware of the fact that he was lying in the shallow water, but instinctively he turned and snapped at the sound of Scat's voice.

'I'm here to help you,' Scat assured him. There was no response, and he continued. 'Your sow is safe, and so are your cubs. They're over at the old mill.'

Slowly, what Scat was saying sank into the badger's tormented mind.

'Hurry,' Scat urged him. 'You must get away while you still have a chance.'

The badger lifted his small head and peered towards the stone. He had been fighting for his life, but without any real hope of keeping it, and now he was hearing a voice that was telling him there was a way. But where was it? 'The pipe's too small,' he heard himself saying. 'It's too small.'

'But the other one's not,' whispered Scat. 'Here, help me shift this stone.'

The badger shuffled over to the stone, and together they managed to move it from the entrance to the pipe. Scat scrambled out and ran to the one opposite. The badger turned and watched. He was dazed and unable to follow what was happening.

'Twinkle,' Scat called softly. 'Twinkle, are you there?'

There was no reply, and he called into the pipe once more. This time he heard Twinkle saying, 'I'm here Scat. I'm here.'

With the badger's help, Twinkle pushed out the second stone, and on Scat's instructions they balanced it on its edge by letting it lean a little against the back wall. Emerging only to turn, Twinkle re-entered the pipe and told the badger to follow her. With surprising alacrity, the badger squeezed in after her and disappeared.

Scat immediately put his shoulder to the stone, and because of the way it was propped up, was able to topple it back into position against the mouth of the pipe without too much effort. He glanced up. So far so good, he thought, and diving into the other pipe, crawled along it as fast as he possibly could.

From his hiding place on the hillside, Young Black Tip was relieved to see Scat emerging from a ditch a short distance from the badger pit. There was no sign of Twinkle or the badger, but he knew the pipe they were in was longer. He just hoped the trapper and his friends wouldn't return to the pit before they got out.   He threw an anxious glance towards the corner of the field.   The men were still there, talking and tending to their dogs.   Then, to his horror, he saw the big dog galloping back down the fields towards them.   It had broken away from the circle of scent he had left for it, and was returning to the trapper!

Young Black Tip stood up.   He hadn't anticipated that the big dog would come back before Twinkle and the badger were clear of the pipes.   He watched as it trotted up to the trapper.   If it stayed there, he thought, they would be all right.

However, he could see it was very unsettled.   Unlike the small dogs, which could only smell the badger blood that still clung to their hair, it had been chasing after another scent — the scent of fox.   It raised its nose to sniff the breeze, and he could see it was confused and curious. Suddenly it was off again, its nose close to the grass as it searched around for any further suggestion of the scent that had been teasing it so much.   Round and round it went. Now it was at the badger pit.   It raised its head, sniffed the air again and barked loudly.

Young Black Tip scanned the ditches for any sign of Twinkle and the badger.   There was none.

The trapper, who was now sitting on a stone smoking his pipe and fingering the fox paw that hung around his neck, looked over at the pit.   He knew well the language of dogs, and when the big one barked again, he took his black terrier and hurried over.

Even from his hiding place on the side of the hill, Young Black Tip could hear the trapper shouting.   He couldn't understand what was being said, but he knew the game was up.   The men were running in different directions, and he guessed that they were rushing to block the ends of the pipes.   His heart sank.   There was nothing he could do.

Seeing that the stone had been pulled away from the entrance to the smaller pipe, the trapper assumed that was how the badger had escaped from the pit.   Having alerted the others, he immediately grabbed a spade and ran down along the ditch to where he knew the pipe came to an end. Kneeling down, he peered inside.   There was no sign of the badger coming out, so he stuffed the end of the pipe with stones and heaped soil in on top of them for good measure. His terrier, which another man was holding for him, was now squealing and barking with renewed excitement. As it strained at the leash, it slobbered at the mouth and the blood lust returned to its eyes.

The man tried to take a firmer grip, but it wriggled free, dashed up along the ditch and bounded over into the pit. Running after it, the man reached the pit in time to see it disappearing into the open pipe.

Meanwhile, the rest of the men had gone to the place where the water entered the larger pipe. It was there they had built a little dam across the stream so that only a trickle of water would flow through the badger pit. Not knowing that the trapper had blocked the other pipe, they immediately released the water with the intention of forcing the badger out of it.

The men were also unaware that Twinkle and the badger were at that very moment still inching their way up through the larger pipe. The progress of the two had been painfully slow, much slower than Twinkle had hoped for. Apart altogether from his injuries, the badger barely fitted into the pipe, and could only move along it with the greatest of difficulty. Indeed, Twinkle realised that had he not lost weight during his captivity, he would not have been able to travel along the pipe at all.

Nevertheless, they were making progress, and were drawing closer to the circle of light that marked the mouth of the pipe, and freedom. Suddenly they heard the sound of man and his dogs, the light darkened, and a wall of water came rushing down towards them. Twinkle closed her eyes and pressed her nose against the roof. The water was all around her. Then it was up to her neck and over her face. She spluttered and gasped for air. The badger, she realised, was blocking the pipe behind her. Memories of the day she was almost drowned in the river below the lake flooded through her mind, and she thought the end had come. She held her breath, spluttered again, and snatched a little more air. Then, almost as suddenly as it had come, the water began to subside.

Twinkle opened her eyes. She could hardly believe that she was still alive, but now she was certain that another nightmare would come true, and that she would be face to face with one of man's savage little fun dogs. To her surprise, she saw that the mouth of the pipe was round and clear again. For some reason, man and his dogs had gone. She could hear the badger snuffling and spluttering behind her. 'Hurry,' she gasped, 'we're nearly out.'

The intention of the men having been to flush the badger out of the other pipe, they had run down to see the results of their handiwork. To their horror, they discovered that the trapper had blocked it, and they were in danger of drowning his terrier inside. They immediately gathered around and as many as could get their hands in, helped him pull the soil and stones away from the mouth of the pipe.

When, a few minutes later, the water gushed out of the pipe, the little black terrier floated out with it. The water had washed the blood from its body, and it was clear to all who saw it that the blood lust had gone from its eyes. It was also clear that the badger had gone, and as the trapper's big dog now put its nose to the ground and set off across the fields, the men assumed it was following the badger's scent. They weren't to know that it had picked up the scent of Scat, and that at that very moment, Twinkle and the badger were emerging from the mouth of the other pipe only a stone's throw away.

Twinkle waited just long enough to see the badger safely out of the pipe, and when it disappeared into the under-growth, she took off along the hedgerows as fast as she could. Young Black Tip, who was still watching from the hillside, was quick to spot her. He raced down across the fields to warn her that the big dog was on the prowl and that it had gone after Scat. Changing course, they made their way to the bog by a roundabout route, and returned to the birches a short time later. Scat, they found, had already arrived.

Little Running Fox and Scab, who had been waiting with mounting anxiety, were now in a high state of excitement, and they danced around them and pawed them in an expression of relief and affection. However, Old Sage Brush bade them be quiet so that he could find out what had happened. He was also very relieved that they had come back safely, but he wanted to hear all the details.

Bit by bit the three cubs related everything that had occurred. As the story unfolded, Little Running Fox and Scab settled down and listened with admiration, while every now and then the old fox nodded his greying head and chuckled with satisfaction, almost as if he had been there himself.

'I didn't even know the big dog was on my trail,' added Scat. 'Once I got clear of the pipe, I put my head down and kept going.'

'So did we,' said Twinkle. 'And you know something else? So did the badger. He never even said thanks!'

'Well, he's alive,' said the old fox, 'and so are you. That's all that matters.'

'I wonder where the badger is now?' asked Little Running Fox.

Twinkle grinned. 'At the rate he was going, he's probably back with his mate and cubs.'

'And I'd say the trapper is still wondering where he went,' said Young Black Tip.

They all laughed, and Old Sage Brush told them, 'Just because the trapper has a paw doesn't mean he can think like a fox.'

The cubs looked at each other and smiled. They knew Hop-along would appreciate that.

10: A Time to Keep

THE BOG WAS TAKING on a purple tinge as the heather came into flower. The cubs had grown a lot since they had come to the birches, and although Old Sage Brush couldn't see them, he knew it wouldn't be long until they entered their second moult and began to acquire the coat that would take them into adulthood. However, that day hadn't quite arrived yet, and while they had acquired a certain amount of wisdom and cunning, they still had a lot to learn.

This was a point the old fox was anxious to impress upon them, and he took the opportunity to do so when Little Running Fox asked one of those questions which only a cub could ask.

'When will we know everything?' she wanted to know.

They were lying beneath the birches talking once more about the rescue of the badger, and he replied in a way that only he could do.

'You will never know everything,' he told her. 'Not even everything you need to know. But, with a little luck, you will know enough.'

'When will that be?' asked Twinkle.

'When you can do the things you cannot do now.'

'Like what?' asked Young Black Tip.

'Well, you know how to fish, but can you catch an eel? You know how to jump, but can you catch a magpie? You know how to run, but can you get rid of the big dog with the stumpy tail?'

The cubs were silent. They had seen eels in the river, but it had never occurred to them how they might catch them.

They had seen how magpies had begun to visit the birches but they were unable to do anything about it. They had seen the trapper's big dog nosing around ever since it had followed Scat from the badger pit, but they had no idea how they might get rid of it.

'Don't fret about it,' said the old fox. 'There are things that even I do not know how to do, and I'm a lot older than you are.'

'Like what?' asked Scat.

'I thought I could cure your brother Scab, but I couldn't.' He sighed. 'Fleas we can drown, lice we can kill, but what are we to do with the mites that are making him itch and waste away. There must be something that will get rid of them. But what is it?'

The others looked at Scab. He was sleeping, as he did a lot of the time now whenever the itch allowed. It had saddened them to see that while they had begun to thrive, he had continued to fail. The itch had become an increasing torment to him. It had left him raw and sore, depressed his appetite to the extent that he was small and thin, and deprived him of much of his coat.

Now as they looked at him and listened to the clacking of the magpies on the edge of the bog, they no longer felt as elated as they had done following the rescue of the badger. They had, of course, felt very proud of their achievement, and so had their parents. But seeing Scab as he was, they suddenly realised that one success didn't solve all their problems. The truth of what Old Sage Brush had said became painfully clear. There were other obstacles to overcome, other things to learn.

It was coming on towards evening, and sensing their change of mood, Old Sage Brush said, 'Come, let's see if we can catch some eels.' He nudged Scab with his nose. 'How about it Scab? Do you fancy a nice juicy eel?'

Scab raised his head, but didn't reply. 'Of course you do,' continued the old fox. 'Come on, the run will do you good. Anyway, the magpies will only torment you if you stay here.'

Slipping out the other side of the birches so that the magpies wouldn't see them, they made their way down to the river, and followed it until they came to a spot where the old fox told them they would find some eels.

'This was always a good place for eels,' he told them. 'They're big too.   Plenty of eating in them.'

As the cubs peered into the river, they could see the dark forms of the eels sliding like shadows across the bottom. They were big all right, they thought, but they were also fast and elusive.   How the old fox proposed to catch them, they couldn't imagine.

'Well?' he asked.   'How do you think we can get them?' There was no reply, and he added, 'I agree, it's not easy.'

The cubs crowded closer, and he told them, 'There's a house not far from here, and every evening the eels go there.'

The cubs looked at each other, thinking the old fox must have taken leave of his senses.

'No, it's true,' he said sensing their doubt, 'they go to the edge of the river at the bottom of the garden.'

'Why should they do that?' asked Young Black Tip.

'Because the woman there feeds them.'

'Feeds them?' said Twinkle.

'That's right.   She gets rid of pieces of chicken and other food she doesn't need.'

'She must like them if she does that,' said Scat.

'Well, maybe she does,' said the old fox.   'But then again, maybe it's just her way of getting rid of her waste.   Sometimes her son will come down and catch an eel, so maybe they like to eat them too, just like ourselves.'

'How does he catch them?' asked Little Running Fox.

'He puts a piece of chicken on a hook and hangs it into the water.'

'And how are we going to catch them?' asked Scat.

'That's what we have to figure out.   But first I better show you where this place is.'

As they made their way farther up-river, the cubs wondered if, perhaps, the old fox knew how to catch the eels, and was waiting to see if they could work it out for themselves. However, if he did, he wasn't telling.

When they came to a spot where the garden of a house ran down to the river, they stopped and the old fox said, 'I think this is it.   Describe it to me.'

'There's a lawn with flowers coming out from the back of

the house,' Twinkle told him. 'Below that is a vegetable garden, and at the end of that the weeds run down to the river.'

'Is there a tree in the garden, with jackdaws perching on its branches?'

'That's right,' said Scat.   'It's got no leaves.'

Taking care not to let the jackdaws see them, they climbed up on to a high patch of ground overlooking the river, and took cover in a clump of weeds.   From there they could see down into the woman's garden.

It was a lovely warm evening, and while they waited, the cubs looked with admiration at the swallows feeding in flight. Sweeping along the river at high speed, they would skim across the water, flutter on the surface for a second to scoop up an insect, and without even losing momentum, streak away again.   All the time they were twittering and screetching, and now and then they would fly up in twos to join together and flap their wings, before swooping down in a high-speed chase.   The young swallows, they could see, were not as expert at flying as their parents, and twittered in a way that signalled a certain degree of insecurity on the wing.

Hearing the cubs talking about them, Old Sage Brush said, 'By the time their tail streamers have grown, they'll be just as good.'   He listened to them twittering and added, 'It won't be long now until they'll be getting ready to leave.   After that, it will only be a matter of time before you will be on your way too.'

The cubs were about to say something when they spotted a kestrel winging its way along the river, closely pursued by a swallow.   To their surprise, they saw the swallow swooping in to attack it.   Each time there was a flurry as the swallow disengaged and then returned to the attack.   However, the kestrel wasn't unduly put out, and continued on up the river.

'I never knew a swallow would attack a hawk,' said Little Running Fox.

'All birds will defend their territory,' the old fox told her. 'Once, before I lost my sight, I saw a wagtail driving off a swallow.   You'd be surprised how fast the wagtail can fly when it wants to.'

'The eels are fast too,' remarked Scat, who had been wondering how they were going to catch them.

'Why can't we just take the chicken?' wondered Young Black Tip.

'We can get chicken any time,' said the old fox, 'and we promised Scab an eel.   Anyway, if you think about it hard enough you might be able to figure out a way to get both.'

Now the cubs were sure Old Sage Brush knew more than he was telling them.

A short time later, the jackdaws took off from the bare ash tree where they had been perching and retreated to the roof of the house.

'That'll be her now,' said the old fox.

The cubs switched their attention to the back of the house, and sure enough they saw the woman coming out and going down the steps to the vegetable garden.   At the edge of the river she took a handful of chicken from a plastic bag and scattered it on the water.

'That will bring the eels up,' whispered the old fox when the cubs told him what she was doing.   'The smell of it will go all the way down the river.'

A few minutes later the woman emptied the remainder of the food into the shallow water at the river's edge, and having waited to see if the eels would venture out from under the stones to take it, she returned to the house.

'Maybe we could catch them if we stood in the water and waited,' suggested Young Black Tip.

Old Sage Brush shook his head.   'They'd see you, and if they didn't see you, they'd smell you.   Even if they didn't, you'd never catch them.'

'They're very fast all right,' said Twinkle.

'They are,' the old fox agreed, 'when they're in the water.'

'Do you mean they come out of the water?' asked Scat.

'Sometimes.   I've seen young eels wriggling up around a waterfall.   And I've seen older ones crawling from one pool to another when the water has been low.'

'So if we could get them out of the water, we'd have no trouble catching them?' said Young Black Tip.

'No trouble at all,' replied the old fox.

'But how could we do that?' asked Little Running Fox.

'Unless we could tempt them out with the chicken,'

suggested Twinkle.

'And get them before they go back,' added Little Running Fox.

'But that way we'd lose the chicken,' protested Scat.

'Would we?' asked the old fox.

The cubs looked at him, and Young Black Tip said, 'You mean, if we got one we'd have the other?'

'Of course.   Wouldn't the chicken be in the belly of the eel?'

The cubs smiled.   As usual the old fox had made it all sound so simple.

Going down to the river's edge, Twinkle and Little Running Fox crept up through a profusion of water mint and purple loosestrife until they were in the garden.   There was no sign of the woman, so they hurried over to where she had thrown the remains of the chicken.

The eels, in their own furtive way, had only come out to snatch a few small pieces, and most of it still lay in the shallow water.   Quickly the cubs retrieved the larger pieces and dropped them into the mud at the water's edge.   Glancing up at the window, they saw that the way was still clear, and tempting though the chicken was, they left it in the mud and hurried back to the others.

When darkness came, all the cubs, with the exception of Scab, went down to the weeds to await the eels.   From the time they had left the birches, Scab hadn't said a word. Now, when he and the old fox were on their own, he squirmed as if he were trying to get out of his skin, and said, 'What am I going to do Sage Brush?   This itch is driving me mad.'

'Scab,' replied the old fox, 'I don't know.   I just don't know.'

Scab rolled over on his back and began to writhe around in the grass.   'It's driving me crazy,' he said.   'I don't think I can suffer it much longer.'

The sound of Scab's agony tore at the heartstrings of the old fox.   Yet there was nothing he could do for him, no advice he could offer, no cure he could give.   'Whatever's doing it, must be under your skin,' was all he could say.

The old fox knew this wasn't much help, but it's doubtful if Scab even heard it.   The itch and the pain of scratching were driving him to the point of desperation.   Suddenly he got up and ran off into the darkness.   Hearing him crashing through the weeds and down the slope towards the river, the old fox called after him, and waited for a reply.   None came.

A few minutes later, the other cubs returned.   They had three large eels in their mouths, and even though they were dead they were twisting and turning around their jaws.

'What happened?' asked Young Black Tip, the only one free to talk as he hadn't an eel.   'I thought I heard you calling.'

'So you did,' said the old fox.   'It's Scab.   He's gone.'

Startled, Scat disentangled himself from the eel that had curled around his nose, and asked, 'Gone?   Gone where?'

Old Sage Brush shook his head.   'I don't know.   The itch is driving him mad.   I don't think he could take it any more.'

'I better go after him and try and keep him out of trouble,' said Scat.

Young Black Tip stepped forward, saying, 'I'll go with you.'

The old fox nodded.   'All right, but you better hurry. He's running wild, and if he doesn't slow down he'll end up in the river or in a choking hedge trap.'

'And what about you?' asked Young Black Tip.

'Twinkle and Little Running Fox will look after me.   Now, off you go and we'll see you back at the birches.'

As the two cubs dashed off into the darkness, Old Sage Brush took Scat's eel, and went with the two vixens back to the bog.

Following Scab's scent, Scat and Young Black Tip found that his headlong flight had taken him down along the bank some distance.   Here and there he had even tumbled into the river, before eventually leaving it and zig-zagging across the fields.   In his madness, they could see he was somehow managing to head for the birches, but not surprisingly, he didn't make it.   On reaching the edge of the bog, they found he had stumbled into a hollow and collapsed in the mud.

'Well, at least he didn't fall into a bog hole,' said Scat, 'or he'd have drowned.'

Between them, they dragged Scab out of the mud and up on to a dry bank covered with long grass and heather. They could see he was exhausted, so they decided to let him rest there during the night. While Scat kept an eye on him, Young Black Tip let the others know what they were doing, and before dawn they got him to his feet and helped him across to the birches.

Almost as if the magpies knew Scab was in trouble, they flew over to the birches at first light. Landing in the flimsy branches, they hopped up and down, chattering and clacking and flicking their long black tails.

Scat glanced up at them. 'You'd think they were trying to tell the whole country we were here.'

'We've got to get rid of them,' said the old fox. 'If the big dog spots them, it'll know we have a problem, and it's making life difficult enough for us as it is.'

Young Black Tip got up, saying, 'I'll draw them off. What about Scab? How is he?'

'He's sleeping at the moment' Scat told him. 'But I think he's all right. He ate the eel anyway.'

'What's going to happen to him?' asked Twinkle.

'He's going to die,' said the old fox. 'If the itch doesn't kill him, the big dog will. That is, if the trapper doesn't catch him first.'

'Are you sure?' asked Little Running Fox.

Old Sage Brush lifted his head in an unseeing glance at the magpies. 'Listen to them. Even they know.'

'Well, I'll draw them off,' said Young Black Tip. 'Then maybe he'll get some peace.'

'Good,' said the old fox, 'but be careful in case the big dog has seen them. And while you're at it, you'd better tell Hop-along and She-la.'

When Young Black Tip left, the magpies followed him. Peace returned to the birches and the others curled up and went to sleep. As they did so, the sun rose and the curlews drifted over the bog, their calls rising and falling with a comforting sweetness which the cubs had come to accept. Suddenly they awoke to find that Young Black Tip had returned. Scab's parents were with him, but to their dismay they also discovered that while they had slept, Scab had run away again.

Scat immediately volunteered to go after him, but She-la said, 'No, leave him be.'

Old Sage Brush was silent, and seeing the look of surprise on Scat's face, Hop-along told him, 'Your mother's right. If the death wish is on him, there's nothing we can do.'

The sun rose higher, and the morning passed. Beneath the birches, the foxes waited. The cubs were hoping that Scab would return. The adults weren't so hopeful, and when they heard the call of a vixen from the hill opposite the bog, they weren't surprised. It was the call of death.

Scat looked at his parents. They nodded, and without a word he and Young Black Tip left the birches and crossed over into the fields. The call, they knew, told of the death of a cub. All that remained was to find out where it had happened and how. The vixen who made the call, directed them to the evergreens, and there, in the hedge that ran around the plantation, they found the body. It was in one of the trapper's snares. The scratched earth and bitten stump to which it was attached, testified to a long and lonely struggle, a struggle which no amount of strength or courage could have won.

Scat looked at the lifeless form and then at Young Black Tip. 'It's not him!' he gasped.

Young Black Tip was also staring at the body. 'It's the young fox we met the day we rescued the badger. He told us the trapper's dog was on the prowl.'

'Where's Scab then?'

Young Black Tip shook his head. 'If the death wish is on him, he'll run until he drops. He could be miles away by now.'

'Death wish or not, I think we should look for him.'

Young Black Tip was still staring at the body of the cub, thinking how full of life he had been the day he had met him. 'First I think we should tell my parents what we've found — in case they don't know the trapper's back in the evergreens.'

Scat agreed, and turning their back on the trapper's grisly work, they raced off through the trees.

When they reached the high bank at the lower end of the evergreens, they found that Black Tip and Vickey weren't at home. However, they alerted Skulking Dog and Sinnéad down at the beeches, and not knowing whether Scab was alive or dead, they hurried away in the hope that they might find him.

Scab, in fact, was still alive and running for his life. At that very moment he was trying to escape, not only from his terrible itch, but from the big dog with the stumpy tail. It had picked up his scent not far from the bog, and was now in hot pursuit.

At the back of Scab's strange behaviour there may well have been an urge to end it all. However, it's more likely that it was simply an urge to end his terrible torment rather than a death wish as such. What is certain is that when he realised the trapper's dog was bearing down upon him, the last thing he wanted to do was die in its jaws.

Had he been in a more rational state of mind, he would have circled around and returned to the safety of the bog, but he wasn't. His body was racked with pain, his mind distraught. All he could think of was to run and keep running, and weak though he was, that is what he did.

Hearing the big dog crashing through a hedge behind him, he stopped momentarily and looked around. Even though it was galloping uphill after him, it was moving easily. He had already begun to tire and he knew instinctively that he wouldn't be able to outrun it.

Changing course, he headed down-hill towards the meadows. At the back of his mind was something Old Sage Brush had said, something about the river. What was it? For a moment his pain was forgotten, but his mind was still blurred. It was the day the old fox had taken them down to the lake to show them how to swim. Now he remembered. They must use the river for many things, he had said. Most important of all, they must use it to escape from man and his dogs. But how could it be used for that? The old fox hadn't told them. Or had he?

Scab was confused. He couldn't think straight. He kept on running, and in the meadows stopped once more to glance back at his pursuer. It was gaining on him. He was turning to go, when he realised he was at the edge of a pond and quickly pulled back. The water was covered with weed so that it was as green as grass. His heart pounded at the thought of taking such a careless step, for he knew he wouldn't have been able to get out in time.   Then, as he started off again, it occurred to him that he might use the pond to slow down the big dog.

Running around to the far side, he paused once more, and when he was sure the dog had seen him, he took off for all he was worth.   A few moments later he smiled as he heard it crashing into the pond.   It was howling now as it wallowed around in the weed-covered water.   Unfortunately, he thought, there was no fear of it drowning.   It would soon struggle out, and be after him again.   He pressed on.

Reaching the river, Scab wondered which way he should go.   If he went down-river it would take him to the lake.   If he went up-river, it would take him close to the small wooded glen where they had sought shelter the day of the badger dig.   He tested the breeze.   It was blowing up-river. He remembered as a very young cub his mother and father telling them that if they were ever chased they should run with the wind as it would carry their scent away from their pursuer.   It was a trick they had learned from Old Sage Brush.   Knowing that any delay, even a moment's indecision, could be fatal, he decided to go up-river, and set off along the bank as fast as he could.

A short distance farther on, Scab found himself at the stone bridge where Old Sage Brush had shown them the little bird that walked on the water.   Stopping again, he looked back and wondered about his ground scent.   What if the big dog picked up that?   The old fox said it had a good nose.   His mind returned to the bird again, and he had an idea.   If it could walk in the water, why couldn't he? Perhaps the water would carry away the scent he left with his paws, just as the wind carried away the scent he left with his body.   He wasn't sure if it would work, but at least, he thought, it might confuse the big dog long enough to give him a head start.

Plunging in, he walked under the bridge and continued up-river as far as he could.   When the water became to deep to walk, he swam a short distance and then returned to the bank.   That should stop the big dog, he thought and shaking the water off himself, he cut across the fields towards the glen.

Clever as they were, Scab's tricks didn't succeed in throwing the big dog off his trail. They confused it all right, just as he had planned, but not for long, and he hadn't gone very far when he found to his dismay that it was catching up on him again. He could see that the fields around the glen, being so highly cultivated, had few if any hedgerows that would give him protection. However, he found that the barley and wheat were high now, high enough to hide him.

Diving in under the first crop he came to, he found that by keeping between the rows he could run quite fast. The trapper's dog, on the other hand, was jumping up and down in an effort to catch a glimpse of him. The result was that he reached the far side of the field first.

It was now or never, he thought, and breaking into the open, he raced up a track between the fields in a last desperate effort to reach the glen. The big dog spotted him immediately, and sensing that it was closing in for the kill, sped after him at full stretch.

There was no way Scab could now match the speed of the dog, and even though they were going up-hill again, the gap between them narrowed with frightening rapidity. He could hear it panting and almost feel its breath on his bare back. He looked up. He was almost there. He couldn't see it, but he knew the big dog was opening its great jaws to take him. In fear and desperation, he put on a final spurt. Where he found the strength, he would never know, but with one last mighty effort he flung himself at a hole in the fence. A flick of his mangy tail, and he was through. He could almost hear the dog's teeth snapping behind him, and then there was a thud as it careered into the fence.

By the time the dog had squeezed through the hole in the fence, Scab was skidding down through the undergrowth like a scalded cat. He wondered where the fox earths were, or the badger sets. There was no sign of them, so he kept going. He could hear the dog crashing after him now, and he feared it would never give up.

Skirting the muddy pond, he ran under the large yew tree with the birds' nests and on past the houses. Children who were playing in front of the houses, screamed as he ran among them and continued on down towards the old mill. Grown-ups came to the doors in time to see a big dog gallop-

ing past and a mangy fox hopping into the weeds at the side of the lane.

Hoping that the water might sweep away his scent once more, Scab entered it where it left the mill and formed a river again. This was the spot just below the waterfall where a white froth floated on the surface, and as he crossed over he wondered if the bubbles might carry his scent downstream.

However, the big dog was too close to be deceived. As he hopped into the old mill, he caught a glimpse of its powerful jaws coming up over the grassy bank after him and he could see from the froth on them that it had followed his trail with unerring accuracy.

From the direction of the houses Scab could still hear the cries of consternation. His natural instinct was to run from man, and he was about to re-enter the undergrowth when he remembered the words of Old Sage Brush the day they had been hunting in that very same spot. Twinkle had come out of the water with froth on her mouth, and they had teased her about it. 'You want to be careful,' the old fox had told her, 'in case man might think you're a mad dog.'

What if the people up at the houses saw the big dog with froth on its mouth? Would they think it was a mad dog, or had the old fox only been joking. Scab had no way of knowing, but he had run out of time, and he reckoned it was worth a try. Circling the old mill, he recrossed the river at the same place, taking good care to go through the foam. The big dog followed, and was hard on his heels as he headed back up towards the houses.

Whatever the people were waiting for, they weren't expecting the fox to return, and when it reappeared among them, they scattered, screaming and shouting, in all directions. For, whatever about the condition of the fox, it was plain to see that the big dog that was hunting it was slobbering and frothing at the mouth. Women grabbed children to lift them out of harm's way, while men grabbed pitchforks and anything else they could lay their hands on.

Scab, of course, didn't know what the people were shouting. Nor did he know whether they were reacting to what looked like a mad dog or a diseased fox. All he knew was that his ploy was having the desired effect. While the dog was trying to corner him, the men were now trying to corner the dog.

Seeing the door of an out-house lying open, he ran inside and climbing up over some bags of foodstuffs, took refuge on top of a dividing wall that didn't quite reach the roof. There he lay, ears flat back, watching intently as the big dog climbed up onto the bags in an effort to get at him.   Then, as it stood barking loudly at him, he dropped down the far side of the wall and raced back out the door.   The men, meanwhile, had gathered around the doorway, and seeing him leave, immediately closed the door to keep the dog inside.

Finding himself free of the big dog at last, Scab left the glen and headed for the bog.   On the way, he ran into Scat and Young Black Tip and they saw him safely back to the birches.   Somehow he had survived another day, but it had been a close thing, and he knew it.

11: A Time to Cast Away

THE LONG SUNNY DAYS had turned the barley fields into patches of gold, and as the first sounds of the combine harvesters carried across the bog, Old Sage Brush cocked an ear and smiled.

The cubs looked at him, puzzled, and Scat said, 'Why do you welcome man's machines to the fields?'

'But do you not hear anything else?' asked the old fox.

'All I can hear is the magpies,' said Young Black Tip.

'Then your ears deceive you, and so do your eyes. When man starts to cut the corn there are more birds in the air, more movement on the ground.'

'And what is there to be happy about in that?' asked Young Black Tip.

'Everything,' the old fox told him. 'You see, a time of plenty for others, means a time of plenty for us. Man's machines will drive the rabbits from the corn, and when they do, we will be waiting for them. The birds will also come in great numbers to feed on the seed, and we will be waiting for them too.'

'What are you waiting for then?' asked Twinkle.

The old fox lifted his head towards the magpies which were clacking loudly in the birches above them. 'We have to get rid of them first.'

'But how?' asked Young Black Tip.

'That is for you to decide, and you must do it soon. Man's machines will gobble up the corn very quickly, and then he will burn the stubble. The time between is best, and sometimes it is very short.'

The magpies had become a great source of annoyance to the foxes, for not only were they drawing attention to them, they had also begun to humiliate Old Sage Brush and Scab.

The other cubs were now beginning to hunt for themselves, and on returning to the birches they sometimes found the magpies playing a teasing game. There seemed to be six or seven in the family, and the largest showed no fear of man or beast. It was as if, being the head of the family, it was continually setting out to prove itself. Thus, when the other cubs had gone, it would descend, followed by its friends, and strutting around would peck at Scab's wounds, or at the tail of the old fox. It was always careful to do it when they were sleeping, and because the two of them were weak, it knew they posed no danger. This greatly angered the cubs, but they were deeply offended when, one day, they came back to find Old Sage Brush walking about the birches with the big magpie riding on his back. Feeble as he was, the old fox was unable to dislodge it, and was forced to suffer the indignity. Young Black Tip soon

shifted it, but it easily evaded his snapping jaws and retreated to the birches with its family, there to berate and abuse them with a continuous raucous chatter.

Young Black Tip was furious. 'That's it,' he declared. 'They've got to go.' The others agreed. They were just as angry, and then as they realised how helpless they were to deal with the magpies, their anger grew. It was the old fox who calmed them down. 'Nothing is ever gained in anger,' he told them quietly.'Nothing, except trouble for yourselves.'

Scat, who was glaring up at the magpies, said, 'I wish I had wings, just for once.'

'But you haven't, have you?' said the old fox. 'However, you have something that the magpies do not have.'

'What's that?' asked Scat.

'Their beak is bigger than their brain – so you have the advantage over them.' The old fox went over to his den near where Scab was dozing and curled up. Seeing that he was leaving them to work the problem out, the four of them went to the opposite end of the birches and lay down.

'He's saying we're smarter than the magpies,' said Twinkle.

'And we should be able to figure out how to get rid of them,' added Little Running Fox.

'It's all very well to talk,' said Young Black Tip. 'But it's easier said than done.'

Scat went over to one of the trees and tried to jump up.

'You're only wasting your time,' Young Black Tip told him. 'They're too straight to climb.'

'We've got to think,' said Twinkle. 'Old Sage Brush was telling us to use our minds, not our strength.'

'Ratwiddle told me how to drive away the stoats,' Little Running Fox recalled. 'Maybe he could tell us how to get rid of the magpies.'

Young Black Tip laughed. 'By the time we figured out what he was trying to tell us, the fields would be on fire.'

Scat agreed. 'A fat lot of help he was the day we went down to the river. We nearly drowned before we found out he was telling us to watch out for the flood.'

Little Running Fox stood up. 'Well, we're not doing any good lying around here. Let's draw them off so that Old Sage Brush and Scab can have a decent sleep.'

'Good idea,' said Twinkle.   'And maybe we should watch them for a while to see if we can come up with something.'

The dog cubs couldn't think of anything better to do, so they agreed.

Having flown ahead of them, the magpies were waiting in a tall ash tree beyond the bog.

'I remember my father saying he caught a magpie once,' said Little Running Fox.

'How?' asked Twinkle.

'I don't know.'   She looked at her brother.   'Can you remember?'   Young Black Tip shook his head.   They were lying under a hedge peering up at the tree.

'Why don't we ask him?' suggested Twinkle.

'All right,' said Little Running Fox, and turning to the dog foxes, told them, 'You two stay here and keep an eye on them.   We'll be back as soon as we can.'

On the way to Beech Paw, Little Running Fox and Twinkle circled around the barley fields.   At one spot they stopped to watch one of man's great machines gobbling up large strips of grain.   Twinkle grinned.   'It's got a huge appetite.'

'And look at the rooks, and all the other birds,' said Little Running Fox.   'They're all over the field.   Old Sage Brush is right.   The sooner we get rid of the magpies, the sooner we can go hunting.'

Farther on they caught a rabbit that had run terrified from the barley field, and Twinkle took it over to her parent's earth at Beech Paw.   'We thought Hop-along might like it,' she told her mother.   Sinnéad smiled.   'That was very thoughtful of you.   But why have you come?'

'The magpies are giving us a lot of trouble,' explained Little Running Fox.   'I remember my father saying he caught one once, and we were wondering how.'

'Well, let's go up and ask him,' said Sinnéad.

Taking the rabbit with them, they made their way up to the high bank at the bottom edge of the evergreens.

Black Tip and Vickey were at home, and were delighted to see them.   'How's Scab?' asked Black Tip.

'Not so well,' replied Twinkle.   'But I suppose he's lucky to be alive.'

'I don't know how he has managed to survive this long,' said Little Running Fox.   'We felt sure he had died in that

choking hedge trap up there in the evergreens.   How come
the trapper has put them out so early anyway?'

'It may be one he put out last season,' said Black Tip.

'And just forgot,' added Vickey.   'I don't think he wants
your fur just yet.   He's more interested in your adult coat.'

'Poor Scab's won't be much use to him,' reflected
Twinkle.   'He's in an awful mess.   And the magpies won't
leave him alone.   Or Old Sage Brush.'

Little Running Fox asked her father about the time he had
caught one of them.

'That was really very simple,' said Black Tip.   'We were
on our journey with Old Sage Brush, and I was out hunting
with Skulking Dog, when some magpies mobbed us.   We
just ignored them, you know, until they came closer, and
then snap, that was it.   I got one.'

'So you didn't have to get rid of all of them,' said Little
Running Fox.

Black Tip shook his head.

'Old Sage Brush says we should be able to do it,' said
Twinkle, 'but we can't just imagine how.'

As she was speaking, Skulking Dog arrived and she told
him about her predicament.

'Maybe you could pick them off one at a time,' he
suggested.

Twinkle looked at her father in a way that indicated she
appreciated his advice but didn't think it was much use.

Sinnéad felt the same.   'They want rid of them all, and
they want rid of them quickly.   If they set out to pick off
one at a time they'll be picked off themselves by the
trapper's big dog.'

'Anyway,' said Vickey, 'if I know Old Sage Brush he wants
them to figure it out, not us.   Isn't that why we sent them
over to him?   So that they can learn how to do things like
that themselves.'   Disappointed though they were, the cubs
knew Vickey was right, and taking the rabbit, they made
their way up along the blackthorns.   Hop-along and She-la
weren't at home, so they left the rabbit just inside the earth,
and turned to go back to the bog.

Little Running Fox stopped.   'You know, I still think we
should ask Ratwiddle.   I mean, what have we got to lose?
And we've no need to tell the others, have we?'

Twinkle giggled. The idea obviously appealed to her, and she said, 'Why not?'

On the way to the river below the dam, they passed through masses of ragwort that had flowered to give the grazing fields a bright splash of yellow. Here and there along the hedgerows, tall spikes of dock sorrel were turning reddish brown, and bindweed had twisted itself up around them to dangle white trumpets in the breeze. The passing season had stripped the flowers from the elder bushes and the rowan trees, to reveal masses of tiny berries, while underneath the hogweed had gone to seed.

Down at the river the cubs concealed themselves in a patch of weeds and waited in the hope of seeing Ratwiddle. For a while they watched black and orange caterpillars climbing the ragwort. The caterpillars were fat, but somehow their colours weren't very appetising. Nor were the host of ladybirds that were also flitting about in the weeds, so they decided to fish with their tails instead.

Not forgetting Ratwiddle's advice the day of the flood, they took good care to keep an eye on the dam. There was no sign of danger and they were beginning to think there was no sign of Ratwiddle either, when a large grey heron flapped up through the trees and winged its way overhead. Ratwiddle appeared a few moments later, his neck stiff and his head twisted, almost as if he was watching the heron with one eye and looking for rats with the other.

He didn't respond to their greeting, but lay down beside them on the river bank. 'What brings you here?' he asked, raising his head and looking at the sky.

'It's Old Sage Brush and Scab,' said Twinkle. 'The magpies are giving them a bad time and we don't know what to do about it.'

'Old Sage Brush is long enough in the tooth to know how to deal with a magpie.'

'But he's getting very old now,' Little Running Fox told him. 'He's not as fast as he used to be, and they're teasing him a lot.'

'Standing on his back and pecking at his tail,' added Twinkle.

'And who's Scab?' asked Ratwiddle.

'Hop-along's cub,' replied Twinkle. 'The one with the itch.'

144 Run Swift, Run Free

As if he had suddenly remembered that he himself had an itch, Ratwiddle began to scratch at his fleas. Instinctively, the cubs took a step back, and as they did, Little Running Fox found she had a minnow hanging out of her tail. Ratwiddle looked down at the wriggling fish with one eye and asked, 'Who showed you how to fish?'

'Old Sage Brush,' she told him.

'Old Sage Brush,' he repeated rather dreamily, and they could see he was drifting off into another world. 'And he can't catch a magpie that pecks at his tail?'

'Maybe he can,' Twinkle hastened to explain. 'But we can't.'

'That's why we came to you,' said Little Running Fox. 'We thought maybe you could tell us how.'

For a moment the cubs thought Ratwiddle wasn't going to reply. Then he said, 'Maybe you should start fishing for magpies.'

That was all the advice he would give, and as they left him to go back to the bog, they didn't know whether to be glad or sorry that they had sought his help.

'Your brother would have a good laugh at us if he knew,' said Twinkle. 'So would Scat. Imagine going back and telling them that they should fish for magpies!'

Little Running Fox smiled. 'I wonder what he meant by that?'

Twinkle shook her head. 'I don't know. Unless he was saying we could use our tails to tempt the magpies — you know, the same way as we do with the fish.'

'Tempt them where? When we land fish they can't get back into the water. But magpies just fly off.'

'It might be simpler if we got Old Sage Brush to move back into an earth,' said Twinkle. 'Then they wouldn't be able to get away so easily.'

Little Running Fox stopped. 'Twinkle, I think you've got it. Only he doesn't need to move back to an earth. All he needs to do is tempt them into one with his tail! We can do the rest.'

Twinkle's eyes lit up. 'Do you think that's what Ratwiddle meant?'

'I don't know, but we could try it. Come on, let's see if we can find some place near the bog that's suitable.'

Soft stars of thistledown, tugged free of their bursting seed heads by feeding goldfinches, drifted across the bog, but the cubs were hardly aware of them. They had eyes only for the dark clouds of smoke that were rising from the barley fields and giving the sky a daytime darkness they had never seen before.

To their surprise, Old Sage Brush wasn't alarmed. 'Man doesn't harvest all his crops in one day,' he told them. 'Nor does he burn all his fields as quickly as that one. Now, what were you saying about the magpies?'

'We think we know a way to get rid of them,' said Twinkle.

'And how's that?'

'There's an old rabbit warren back up the fields a bit,' explained Little Running Fox. 'The bank is really riddled with holes, and we thought that maybe you could tempt them into it with your tail.'

The old fox grunted and smiled.

'But it might work,' protested Twinkle. 'All you have to do is get them to follow you. We'll do the rest.'

'Oh I'm not saying it won't work,' said the old fox. 'I'm just laughing at the idea. How did you think of it?'

Little Running Fox looked at the dog cubs and said, 'Twinkle and I were just talking about it. We thought that if we could catch fish with our tails, why couldn't we do the same with magpies.'

'And what about the rest of you?' asked the old fox. 'Are you leaving it all to the vixens?'

'It sounds like some daft idea Ratwiddle would dream up,' said Young Black Tip. The vixens looked at him, but didn't say anything, and he added, 'I don't know, it might work.'

'Scat?'

Scat shrugged. 'I suppose it's worth a try.'

'Scab?'

'He's asleep,' said Twinkle.

Old Sage Brush got up. 'All right. No need to disturb him. Now am I right in thinking the magpies are in the bushes at the edge of the bog?'

'Are they ever anywhere else,' said Young Black Tip, 'if they're not over here.'

'Right. Let's see if they still have a taste for my tail.'

Old Sage Brush told the cubs to go ahead, saying he

would follow. He knew the fields around the bog well enough to find his way to the rabbit warren alone. He also knew the magpies well enough to know that if he walked very slowly, they would follow him. And so they did.

Had man been present and patient enough to watch, he would have witnessed the strange sight of a weak old fox walking up the fields, with one large magpie riding on his back and several others flitting around, pecking at his drooping, moth-eaten tail. But, like so many other things in the wild that go unseen, there was no one around to see it.

The cubs were keeping an eye on the old fox's progress, and as he drew the magpies closer to the warren, Little Running Fox ran up the back of the hedge and joined the others inside. The bank was so honeycombed with burrows it was almost falling in, and this suited them perfectly as there were plenty of places where they could hide inside.

When he arrived at the warren, the old fox didn't go into it right away. Instead he lay down just outside it, as if to rest. There he waited and suffered the magpies until he was absolutely sure that even the youngest of them had no fear of him. Then he got up and slowly made his way into the warren, and in spite of the nips he was getting he had to smile at the thought of catching magpies with his tail!

The magpies, of course, had no idea what was in store for them. The largest and most adventurous fought with the others to be the first to follow, and while it may not have been its intention to follow very far, it went far enough. Just inside the burrow, one of the cubs was waiting in a side tunnel, and its death was so sudden and so silent that the others, which were still flapping around the entrance, were unaware of what was happening.

Even though he couldn't see, Old Sage Brush knew exactly what was happening. Without pausing he went out the other side and came back through the hedge. The magpies immediately began to mob him again, and when he went into the burrow once more, another followed him, only to meet the same fate. Thus the cubs disposed of the magpies one by one, and when, a short time later they returned to the bog, it was with considerable satisfaction that they reflected on what they had done. For not only had they rid themselves of their tormentors, they had filled their stomachs at the same time.

'Even the last one didn't notice it was on its own,' laughed Twinkle.

'Maybe it thought the others were all inside,' said Young Black Tip.

'So they were,' grinned Scat, and Little Running Fox added, 'Inside the warren, and inside us!'

The old fox was content to listen. He didn't say anything, but they knew what he was thinking, for he had said it before.   The magpie's beak was bigger than its brain.

The harvest was now in full swing, and having got rid of the magpies, the foxes were freer than they had been for a long time to come and go as they pleased.   There was always the possibility that the trapper's big dog would still see them, but with caution they could avoid it.   At least they had the comfort of knowing that the magpies were no longer around to tell it where they were.   Because the barley fields in the area of Beech Paw were either scorched or aflame, they had to hunt farther away.   They found that the harvesting was only beginning in some places, and in others had not begun at all.   They also found to their great disappointment, that many of the rabbits that lived around these cornfields were suffering from their sleepy sickness again.   Fortunately there were other things to hunt.

Sometimes Scab would go along, but even if he did he wasn't always with them in spirit.

'He's getting as bad as Ratwiddle,' said Young Black Tip during one hunting expedition.   'If he's not scratching and rolling around, he's dashing off on his own.'

Scat had to agree.   'He's gone beyond the stage where you can talk to him.   But as long as he keeps quiet I suppose he's not doing any harm.'

Young Black Tip wasn't so sure.   Scab's antics were making them all a bit jumpy, and they were finding it difficult enough to hunt.

In his heart, Scat realised this, so he said, 'Look, I tell you what.   You go ahead with the others.   I'll stay here and keep an eye on him.'

Twinkle had spotted two kestrels hovering over a nearby field of stubble, and come back to tell Old Sage Brush about it.   'Whatever's in it, they have it,' she said.

The old fox, however, had other ideas.   'Why should they have it?'

'You mean we should go in and take it from them?' inquired Little Running Fox.

'Maybe.   First we have to find out what they're after.'

Having left Scat to look after his brother, Young Black Tip was peering through the hedge into the field.   'It's birds of some sort,' he whispered.   'They're running through the stubble.' Twinkle, who was also watching the movement in the stubble, added, 'They seem to have a little tuft on their head.'

'Hmm, just as I thought,' said the old fox.   'Larks.'

'If we rush in they'll all fly off,' said Little Running Fox.

'I told you before.   Never rush into anything.   Only fools do that.   Anyway, why go to all that trouble?'

'How else are we going to get them?' asked Twinkle.

'That should be obvious,' replied the old fox.   'The kestrels can't land on the stubble, and the larks can't fly out of it.   They're on the run, and when they appear we'll be waiting for them.   So relax.   Let the kestrels do the work.'

Slowly the kestrels fluttered and hovered as they followed the larks down the field.   Their wings were fully out-stretched, their black-banded tails fanned out, their heads bent downwards watching their prey.

'Careful in case they see you,' warned the old fox.   'Their eyes are as good as ours, if not better.'

The kestrels were coming closer now, and the cubs could see that while they were continually making small adjust-ments of their wings and tails, their heads were absolutely still.   The cubs switched their gaze to the edge of the stubble and waited for the larks to appear.   Suddenly the kestrels veered away and the larks broke into flight.

'It's Scab!' exclaimed Young Black Tip.   'He's off again.'

Looking to the left, the vixens saw Scab racing wildly through the stubble field, closely followed by Scat.

'Let them go,' said Old Sage Brush.   'There's nothing we can do for them.'   He sighed.   'And there's nothing more we can do here.'

As the others followed the old fox back to the bog, Scab continued his mad dash across the fields with Scat in

pursuit.   Soon they had left the stubble field far behind,
and Scat was wondering what he would do if he caught up
with his brother.   Maybe, he thought, he would wrestle
with him, and try and knock some sense into his head.   If
only he *could* catch up with him.   He wasn't even sure of
being able to do that.   The agony in Scab's body was
driving him on at a crazy speed.   What was more, he was
heading for the evergreens again.

On and on they ran, until it seemed they were running
away from the day and into the night.   For as they neared
the evergreens, clouds of black smoke obscured the sun and
darkened the sky.   Scat looked up.   Beneath the swirling
smoke he could see rooks and other birds flying away and
he guessed that new fires had been started.   Scab, on the
other hand, seemed oblivious to anything that was going on
around him, and had no idea that he was running towards
the fires.   Occasionally he would fall and roll over, but each
time he picked himself up and kept going.

Now, to make matters worse, Scat spotted the trapper's
big dog.   It was roaming around a field to his left.
Unfortunately his brother had thrown caution aside and was
running in a straight line.   There was no question of
circling, no time to turn.   As they passed, the big dog lifted
its head, and seeing them, bounded after them.

Pressing on, Scat could see the shadowy figure of Scab
disappearing into the smoke.   He glanced up.   The smoke
was drifting low over him now, and he reckoned they
weren't far from where the stubble was being burned.
Soon the smoke was all around him.   The air was filled
with sparks and flecks of ash.   He looked back.   He could
just make out the big dog casting about, searching for
them.   Ahead the smoke was thick and black.   His eyes
were smarting and he could hardly breathe, but there was
nothing for it but to keep going.   He could feel the stubble
under his paws now.   Tongues of flame ran here and there,
crackling the straw and reducing it to black ash and smoke.
Dark shapes loomed up, men, raised sticks, waving arms.

Scat was wondering which way to turn when another
shape came charging through the gloom.   For a moment he
thought it was the dog, and to his relief he saw it was
Scab.   He was running this way and that, and Scat knew he

was completely unaware of where he was or what was happening. There were shouts, barks. Waving shapes came and went. Suddenly Scab was on the ground, writhing around on his back, trying to extinguish the pain from his body. Then he was on his way again, flaming straw sticking to his scabby back and tail.

Seeing him hurtling off into the smoke, Scat flung himself after him, and to his surprise found he was out in the fresh air. He stopped. Flames licked around his paws. Scab was streaking across the blackened field towards the evergreens, smoke trailing from his back. There were shouts and he knew they had been spotted. He took off. Hot ash stung his pads, spurring him on to even greater effort, and he reached the evergreens only seconds after Scab. Pausing just inside to get his breath, he looked back. The big dog was galloping across the field after them. He hurried on, and towards the far side of the evergreens, found Scab rolling around beneath the trees.

'Come on Scab,' he panted, 'the big dog's on our trail.'

Scab got up. He had extinguished the flames on his back and tail, but somehow, he found, he had transferred them to the dry pine needles that carpeted the ground. Even as he watched, the flames began to spread and grow bigger. He jumped to one side, for he now associated the flames with pain, and in an instant he was gone again.

With one look at the flames, which were now leaping up through the trees, Scat followed. Out into the open fields they ran, and on down across the hill until they reached the river below the dam. There Scab plunged in and allowed the water to quench the pain that burned along his back and tail. When, a few moments later, he came back out, he appeared to be calmer, almost as if the water had had a soothing effect upon him.

'Look what you've done,' whispered Scat.

Scab looked up across the hill to see the evergreens flaring up in one huge tongue of flame. 'Did I do that?' he asked.

Scat was looking at the fire with increasing awe. Fanned by the breeze, the flames were roaring through the evergreens with frightening speed. 'I think you must have,' was all he could say.

'It's much bigger than the one man made in the corn field,' said Scab.

Scat smiled.   The evergreens were now a raging inferno, and not quite sure how they should react to it, said, 'Come on, we better get back to the bog.'

It was several days before the ashes of the evergreens ceased to smoulder.   The flames had forced Black Tip and Vickey to move to another earth, but they didn't mind. While the evergreens had given them shelter when they needed it, the undergrowth around the edges had concealed the trapper's snares.   Now the snares were laid bare, plain for all to see.   Anyway, as they said themselves, the most important thing was that the cubs were safe.

The trapper's dog also had survived the flames. However, the mites which had burrowed into Scab's skin had not.   The burns caused him considerable pain at first, but as the pain disappeared, so gradually did the terrible itch which had tormented him for so long.   And strange as it may seem, the demise of the mites gave them all much more satisfaction than they would have got from the death of the dog.   Somehow or other they felt they could cope with the dog.

12: A Time to Keep Silence

AUTUMN ARRIVED, the wheat ripened and the last of the grain was harvested. The days were still sunny, but there was an unmistakable feeling in the air that the sun's warmth was almost spent. It had ripened the corn and reddened the fruit, but it wasn't shining as strongly as it used to do, or as long. Gradually the darkness was coming earlier, and for the first time the cubs saw the Great Running Fox in the Sky leaping down to touch the hills. While man knew this particular group of stars as the Plough, the foxes considered its shape to be very much like their own, with the last three stars forming the tail. Thus they had their own name for it.

'First you see it coming down,' Old Sage Brush told them. 'Then, some night as darkness falls, you will see it starting to take off. That is when you will know it is time to go.'

'When will that be?' asked Young Black Tip.

'Soon,' said the old fox. 'Soon.'

The cubs still had that young, inquiring look in their eyes and their ears still seemed too big for their faces. But they were now acquiring their adult coat, and Old Sage Brush knew it wouldn't be long before they were indistinguishable from their parents. This was especially so of Twinkle and Young Black Tip, he imagined. She would be the image of her mother, for she would retain the small white star on her forehead, while he would keep the black hairs on the tip of his tail, just like his father. Scab, of course, would never grow a full coat. His scars would always mark him out and set him apart from other foxes. Nevertheless, he was now in the full of his health. At long last he was thriving, and above all was enjoying life as much as the others. The trapper's big dog would still hunt him, but his coat would never be one the trapper would envy.

As the cubs had grown, so also had their appetite. While the stubble fields which had escaped burning, continued to provide a plentiful supply of rats, mice and small birds, the sleepy sickness had almost wiped out the rabbits and substantial amounts of food were becoming difficult to find.

'That is why the young must always find territory of their own,' explained Old Sage Brush. 'We work hard to bring our numbers back up after the trapper has done his work, but then food becomes scarce. Even when rabbits are plentiful, food can be a problem.'

'Will we all have to go?' asked Twinkle.

'Not unless you want to. The dogs yes, but the vixens can stay if they wish. That is the way it is. That is the way it always has been.'

'Meantime, we must find food,' said Young Black Tip.

'The blackberries are ripening,' said Little Running Fox. 'They're lovely.'

'We can't live on blackberries,' replied her brother.

'Maybe not,' she said, 'but the mice live on them, and we can live on the mice.'

Scab agreed with Young Black Tip. 'We need something more substantial than that.'

Old Sage Brush smiled. Since Scab had recovered, his appetite had grown enormously. 'There must be hares in the meadows,' he suggested. 'Why not go after them.'

'They're fairly scarce too,' Scat told him. 'Anyway, they're not easy to catch.'

'It depends on how you go about it,' said the old fox. 'Come on, let's see what we can find.'

It wasn't very often now that they all went out together, for while the cubs had grown, so also had the dangers. However, they enjoyed each other's company, and rightly or wrongly still felt a degree of safety in numbers.

Trotting along the hedgerows, they could see that the elderberries were hanging heavily in bunches of green, red and black. When they ripened, the tell-tale droppings of the starling would be dyed with purple, and the cubs would know that like themselves, the birds had begun to look for other sources of food. The rowanberries would be ripe then too, but at the moment they were a bright orange colour as they changed from green to red.

The brambles were still in flower, although the flowers seemed to have lost their lustre, and bees and small beetles searched among their fading petals for any goodness that might remain. Here and there, where the blackberries were ripe, the cubs stopped to nibble at them. The clusters of hips on the dog rose were green and in one field where the farmer had cut a hedge, Twinkle nibbled at them to see what they were like.

Hearing her spitting them out, Old Sage Brush told her, 'The rose hips are of no use to us, but look carefully and you may see something else that is.'

Taking good care to keep clear of the sharp, hooked thorns, the others crowded around. 'All I can see are two small hairy nests on the stems,' said Twinkle.

'Hairy, yes,' said the old fox. 'Nests? Well, I suppose you might call them that. In fact, they are quite hard. Try one. With luck you will find some grubs inside.'

What, in fact, the cubs were looking at was the home of the grubs of the gall wasp. Twinkle took one of the galls in her mouth and chewed it, but because of its hairy covering, wasn't quite sure if she like it, or indeed, if there was anything in it at all. Scab tried the other one, but didn't fare much better. Old Sage Brush chuckled to himself as they tried to clear the hairy strands from their mouths. 'I suppose you have to develop a taste for them,' he said. 'They're what you might call a delicacy.'

Scab turned to the others and smiled, saying, 'Delicacy or not, I'd rather have a rabbit any time.'

'Or a hare,' added Young Black Tip. 'Anyway, I thought that's what we were looking for.'

'So it is,' said Old Sage Brush. 'But you won't find them here. It's in the meadows you should be looking.'

It was only then that the cubs realised the old fox was waiting for them to lead the way, not the other way round. Strangely, however, there was no sign of any hares in the meadows either, so they continued on towards the foot of the hills. On the way they approached a road and were viewing it from a safe distance to see if it was clear, when a horseman came into sight with a pack of hounds.

'I've never seen so many dogs,' whispered Little Running Fox.   'I wonder if they're howling dogs?'

'How can they be howling dogs if they're not howling?' said Scat.

'What are they like?' asked Old Sage Brush.

'Brown and white,' Twinkle told him.   'They've big noses and floppy ears.'

'And their tails are sticking straight up,' said Little Running Fox.   'Like reeds waving in the breeze.'

'They're tied in pairs,' observed Young Black Tip.

'And the man on the horse?   What about him?'

'Nothing special,' said Young Black Tip.   'His coat's not the colour of blood, if that's what you mean.'

'What do you make of it?' asked Twinkle.

'They're the howling dogs all right,' said the old fox.   The cubs took a step back.   'But don't worry.   They're not out hunting.   The young ones are just being shown how to keep together.   That's why they're chained to the older dogs. Anyway, remember what you were told about the fear of the fear.   There's nothing wrong in being afraid.   Sometimes you think all the better for it.   But if you're afraid of being afraid, you'll never face the world on your own.'

'Now,' he added, 'there's no point in taking risks we don't have to take.   Our scent must be strong, and their nose is second to none.   So I suggest that two of you, maybe Young Black Tip and you Scab, continue on your own and see if you can locate any hares.   The rest of us will go back to the bog.'

'Will you be all right?' asked Young Black Tip.

'Of course we will,' said Scat.   'Just you bring back a good big hare.'

'Better still,' suggested Little Running Fox, 'bring back two.'

Young Black Tip and Scab waited until the howling dogs had disappeared along the road, and the others were safely out of their reach.   Then they crossed the road and made their way up into the foothills in search of hares.

It wasn't until they came to a large flat rushy field that they found one.   It was sitting in the middle of the field, ears erect, its large brown eyes alert for any sign of danger.

'Wait until it starts to eat,' whispered Scab.   'Then we'll move in on it.'

'We'll never catch it that way,' said Young Black Tip. 'They're too fast.   Why don't you make your way around to the far side.   That way you can cut it off.'

'Good idea,' replied Scab, and off he went.

Young Black Tip waited patiently until he saw Scab was in position.   By this time the hare had begun to hop around, nibbling here and there at the grass.   Remembering what Old Sage Brush had told them about not rushing into things, he slipped through the hedge and walked quietly out into the field.   Whenever the hare sat up to look around, he pretended not to be looking at it.   But when it started eating again, he gradually changed direction so that he was veering towards it.   In this way he was getting quite close when, out of the corner of his eye he saw two dogs streaking towards him.   For a moment he thought it was the howling dogs but they were quite different from the ones he had seen on the road.   These were long and skinny and were moving across the field towards him at an astonishing speed.   Indeed, their speed was such that by the time he took all this in, they were almost on top of him.   The hare, he knew, was also caught unawares, and as the two dogs bore down on them, their heads close to the ground, their sharp pointed teeth bared for the kill, it was galvanised into action in the very same instant he was.

Which of them, the strange dogs were after, Young Black Tip had no way of knowing.   But as he raced away he became aware of them splitting up, one veering towards the hare, the other towards himself.   He could hear its paws thudding across the soggy ground behind and he could almost feel its long neck stretching out towards him as it followed his every twist and turn.   It was so close that he couldn't even risk looking around to see which way he might go, but somehow he knew the hedge was too far away.   With a flick of his brush, he did the sharpest turn he had ever done, and was relieved to hear the dog skidding past.   Seconds later, it was on his tail again.   Another sharp turn, and he had another short breathing space.

All this, Scab observed from the side of the field, and as he watched, horrified, he knew exactly how Young Black Tip must be feeling. He had gone through it all with the trapper's big dog, the one with the stumpy tail. But fast and all as that was, it couldn't compare with these creatures. He looked around. There was a rabbit burrow in the bank behind him. 'Over here,' he barked. 'Over here.'

Hearing his call, Young Black Tip ran towards him. The dog was catching up again. He swerved, turned, twisted and doubled back. The rabbit burrow opened up before him, and he dived inside. Outside he could hear the dog thudding up against the entrance, but he knew he was safe.

'Good work,' cried Scab. 'I didn't think you were going to make it.' Young Black Tip lay panting in the darkness beside him. 'What sort of dog was that?' he gasped.

'I don't know. I've never seen anything like it.' Creeping to the entrance, Scab was surprised to see that the dog had suddenly lost interest in them and was galloping back towards its master. The man ran towards it and quickly put it on a leash. A moment later he had the other one back on its leash too, and walked away with them. 'It's the trapper,' he exclaimed. 'He's taking them away.'

Young Black Tip followed him outside. He was still out of breath and shaking like a leaf. 'They must be the ones Twinkle saw,' he panted. 'The night she went over to his house. Remember, when she nearly got poisoned?'

'I think I heard her talking about them all right,' said Scab. 'But I didn't know they were like that.'

'I wonder if they got the hare.'

Scab shook his head. 'It got away through a gap in the hedge. I think the dog gave up.'

'Good. Let's see if we can find it.'

Making sure they weren't being followed, they picked up the scent of the hare and tracked it to a clump of grass in a field some distance away. To their surprise, it didn't move when they approached. It was crouching in a sort of nest and was shaking, just as Young Black Tip had been.

'Are you going to kill me?' it asked.

The cubs looked at each other, and then at the hare. It was a young jack hare, and he was having a severe attack of what Old Sage Brush might call the fear of the fear.

'No,' replied Young Black Tip. 'We're not going to kill you — not if you tell us what's going on. Where have all the other hares gone?'

The hare looked at Scab's scarred back and tail, and asked, 'What happened you? Did the gazehounds catch you?'

Scab smiled, saying, 'Not likely. They'd have a job getting their teeth into my fur. But is that what you call them, gazehounds?'

The hare nodded, a trembling sort of nod.

'How come?' asked Scab.

'Because they hunt with their eyes, not their nose. When they're chasing us they never take their eyes off us, and man never takes his gaze off them.' The hare shivered and sighed. 'It's not as if man wants to catch us for food. Sometimes he just throws our bodies away. I think he just likes looking at the gazehounds running after us.'

The cubs found this very strange, and Young Black Tip asked, 'Is that where all the other hares have gone? Have the gazehounds killed them?'

'Not yet,' replied the hare, 'but they will, given time. Man has been rounding them up for several days now. When he has enough, he will set the gazehounds on them. That will be the end for many of them. You saw yourselves how fast the gazehounds are.'

The cubs nodded, and wondered what satisfaction man could possibly get from gazing upon such animals. The way they were built, they seemed perfectly suited for killing. But just to gaze upon them while they were doing so, was something they couldn't understand. Killing for food was something they could accept. Killing for sport was beyond their comprehension.

Neither the foxes nor the hares could know that over the years man had gone to extraordinary lengths to develop this strange animal which the hares called the gazehound. By crossing it with other dogs, he had given it a broad chest, long sinuous legs and lean body, all designed to provide it with the heartroom, strength and speed that would match the hare. And for extra measure, he had given it a long neck so that it could reach out and more easily make the death strike.

> *Headed like a snake, Necked like a drake . . .*
> *Tailed like a rat and footed like a cat.*

These were some of the qualities which this perfect animal was said to have; being remarkable for its sight and speed, it was also once known to man as the gazehound. Nowadays he called it the greyhound, but it made no difference. The hound was the same, and more often than not so was the fate of the hares.

Young Black Tip asked the young jack hare if he would show them where the other hares were being rounded up.

Not quite knowing if he could trust the foxes, but realising that he really didn't have much choice, the hare agreed.

And so, with the cubs running on either side of him, he led them to a hillside some distance away. There he stopped, turned his head to one side so that he could squint down at the meadows, and told them, 'The last time I saw them, they were being driven down there.'

Focussing their eyes on the meadows, the cubs could see two lines of men moving through them. They were waving their arms as they walked, and a number of hares were running ahead of them. The hares didn't appear to know where to go, or what to do. Now and then they would stop and look around. The men kept coming and gradually the hares were herded towards a gateway in the corner of one particular field. Suddenly they made a break for it. However, they hadn't seen the net strung across the opening, or the men crouching down behind the hedges on either side. Even from the distance of the hillside, the cubs could see them struggling in the nets, and the men running out from behind the hedges to seize them.

The men put the struggling hares into long boxes with bars on the sides, and as they were carried away, Scab asked, 'Where are they taking them?'

'There's a field, over there beyond the hill,' said the young hare. 'They will be put into that. It's fenced in, and later man will bring the gazehounds to chase them.'

'Do many get killed?' asked Young Black Tip.

'Too many.'

'So that's where all the hares are going,' said Scab, more to himself than to anyone else.

Hearing him, the young hare said, 'Not all of them. There's another meadow where man has herded many more. One by one they will be allowed out, but if they out-run the gazehounds they will be free.'

'What's the difference in the two places?' asked Scab.

'In the place where they are fenced in, they may out-run the gazehounds — if they are lucky — but they will be kept to run another day. In the other place, there are no fences, just an open field, and if they escape the jaws of the gazehound, they can return to the hills.'

'And what are their chances of that?' asked Young Black Tip.

The young hare shivered. 'Not good.' He hopped

forward a little bit as if he had suddenly remembered he was in the company of foxes.   'Anyway, why should you worry what happens to us?'

The cubs realised they couldn't tell him it was because they were short of food, and they were almost at a loss for words, when Young Black Tip remembered what Old Sage Brush had told them in the glen.   'Man's upsetting the balance of things,' he said, 'and we don't like it any more than you do.'

The hare didn't quite know what was meant by this, but it sounded sensible enough, so he said, 'There's nothing we can do about it.'

'Maybe nothing you can do,' said Scab. 'But perhaps there's something we can do.'

'Like what?'

'I don't know,' Scab confessed.   'But there is a friend of ours who is very wise.   We can ask him.   Where will we find you if we want you?'

'I'll be here.'   The young hare turned to go, and sensing now that these two foxes at least posed no threat to him, added, 'If you do come back, it might be safer to come at night.   The gazehounds don't hunt at night.'

The moon was big and bright.   It bathed Beech Paw in a soft yellow glow, and as man slept the foxes talked.   Old Sage Brush had called a meeting beneath the circle of beeches where all important matters were discussed and decided. For the foxes, nothing was more important than food.   Food meant survival.   Man had deprived them of much of their food.   First he had burned the stubble, then he had netted the hares.   Now, the cubs heard, he had also given them another mouth to feed when they could least afford to do so.

Vickey informed the old fox that a vixen had sought refuge at Beech Paw.

'What happened?' he asked.

'Her cubs were dug out and thrown to the howling dogs.'

Shocked at this news, the cubs sat up with a start.

'She was lucky to escape herself,' said Sinnéad.   'She's in a state of shock.'

Old Sage Brush sighed, and realising that they were prob-ably the same dogs they had met on the road, said, 'Man

doesn't wait long, does he?   Once they are old enough to
run with the pack, he has to give them a taste of blood.'

There was a silence for a moment, and then She-la said,
'The question is, do we let her stay?   Food is scarce enough
already in this area.'

Coming from anyone else, this might have sounded sel-
fish, but the others knew that She-la's real concern was not
for herself.   It was for her mate.   Because of his handicap,
Hop-along found it difficult enough to catch food, even
when there was plenty of it.

'The question is, do we let her go?' said the old fox.

'What do you think?' asked Vickey.

The old fox raised his grey head and listened, as he often
did, to the rustle of the wind in the leaves.   Then, after
some thought, he replied, 'If man has shown her no mercy,
does that mean we must do the same?'

She-la got up, anxious that what she had said should not
be misunderstood.   'No, of course not.   It's just that sometimes I wonder if we will find enough food to go around.'

'She-la,' said the old fox gently, 'you worry too much.   If
Hop-along can find enough with three legs, then the rest of
us can manage on four.   Anyway, Vulpes will provide.
Now, talking of food, what can we do about the hares?'

The cubs, lying beside their parents, listened in
silence.   It was the first time they had attended this council
of elders, and as yet none of them had dared to speak.

'There is no way we can take them from the gazehounds,'
said Skulking Dog.   'If man has them, then that's the end
of it.'

Black Tip agreed, and plucking up the courage to speak,
his dog cub said, 'They're fast all right.   Scab and I were
lucky to get away from them.'

Sinnéad nodded.   'Skulking Dog was able to out-run the
howling dogs when he rescued me, but even he could not
out-run the gazehounds.   The hares can hardly do it, and
we all know how fast they are.'

'They could out-run them if they weren't so stupid,' said
Vickey.

Little Running Fox looked at her mother, wondering what
she meant.

'I saw them from a distance once,' Vickey explained,

'when they were being chased in the open field above the meadows.   What they have in speed, they lack in cunning.'

'That's a thought,' said the old fox. 'Do you think perhaps we could teach them a trick or two?'

'I doubt it,' said Black Tip.   'But maybe we could give them a few hints.'

'Don't forget,' Hop-along told them, 'a lot of their trouble comes from the fact that their eyes are in the sides of their heads and they've a blind spot in front.   That's why they run into man's nets so easily in the first place.'

'But if they have a blind spot in front of them,' said Vickey, 'doesn't that mean they could lead the gazehounds into the blinding light of day and not be blinded themselves?'

Old Sage Brush nodded.   'They have a blind spot all right, but sometimes I think it's between their ears as well as their eyes.   Anyway, if they have the wit to do it, I suppose it would be a start.'

'I've noticed the gazehounds are inclined to trip on any patch of water they cross,' said Black Tip.

'And they tire quicker than the hares,' added Skulking Dog.

'If only the hares would head for the nearest gap in the hedge and keep going,' said Vickey.   'Somehow they seem to prefer to say in the wide open field, and that's where the gazehounds catch up with them.'

Old Sage Brush got up, saying, 'All right.   Let's tell them what they're doing wrong, and what they can do to get it right.'   He smiled.   'Scab, Young Black Tip, that will be your job.   When gloomglow comes again, return to the hills and when you find the young hare, ask him to pass on our advice to his friends.   But be careful you don't tell him too much.   We don't want them to know how to get away from us!'

As they turned to go, Vickey called after them, 'And stay away from the gazehounds.   We don't want to give them a taste of our blood too.'

13: A Time to Hate

A YELLOWED LEAF fluttered down from the birches and landed on Young Black Tip's nose. He awoke to find that a misty dawn was spreading across the bog. Everywhere, drops of dew were clinging to the threads of spiders' webs like strings of tiny translucent pearls. It was only now, when the webs were etched so clearly in the morning mist, that he could see how many and varied they were. Somehow it was almost as if he was seeing them for the first time. Close by, an orb web spider had spun its large, yet fragile net between tall stalks of weeds and heather, and as he marvelled at the way it was made, he couldn't help thinking that spiders caught flies in much the same way as man caught hares. Giving Scab a nudge, he whispered, 'You know, there's no way the flies can escape.'

Scab yawned. 'What are you talking about?'

'I'm talking about the hares. We'll starve if we wait for them to find their own way out. I mean, how do we know they'll take our advice? And even if they do, they still may not be able to get away from the gazehounds.'

'What else can we do?'

'I don't know, but we'll have to do something — and I'm not going to lie around here until gloomglow thinking about it.'

'But your mother said to stay away from the gazehounds.'

'They said a lot of things up there last night, but they didn't really decide to do anything. Come on. Let's find the young hare now and see what we can do.'

Seeing that the others were still asleep, they slipped silently out of the birches, and picking their way around the glistening array of spiders' webs, left the bog as quietly as the mist itself would leave.

In common with the other cubs, Young Black Tip and Scab had listened carefully to all that had been said under Beech Paw, and on returning to the birches had talked about it long into the night. They knew well that they could not out-run the gazehounds, but they also felt that somehow the meeting had been very indecisive.

Nothing definite had been arranged to recover the hares, and they doubted if the hares would be able to do much for themselves. They were, as Young Black Tip remarked again on their way to the hills, almost as helpless as the flies in the spiders' webs.

Sensing that his friend had something in mind, Scab said, 'We must be careful we don't walk into a trap ourselves.'

'How do you mean?'

'Well, if it's an open field where the gazehounds are chasing the hares, then what's to stop them chasing us, the way they did the last time we were up here?'

'But the hare said there was another place, a place where they were fenced in.'

'And what about it?'

'Well, if the hares are fenced in so that they can be chased, then the gazehounds must be fenced in too.'

Young Black Tip seemed sure of what he was saying, but Scab wasn't so certain. Perhaps it was his encounters with the trapper's other dog, the one with the stumpy tail, that had left him less than enthusiastic about taking on the gazehounds. 'We're even taking a risk coming here now,' he said. 'The hare said to come when it was dark and so did Old Sage Brush.'

'I know, but I was afraid Sage Brush might twig on to what we were at. That's why I wanted to get away before he woke. Anyway, we know what to look out for now.'

'And what about the howling dogs?'

'Come on,' said Young Black Tip. 'They wouldn't know you were a fox even if they did see you. And neither would the gazehounds. Why do you think it was me they chased the last time?'

Scab smiled. What could he say?

Joking apart, they kept a sharp look-out for danger as they

continued on up into the hills. In roughly the same area, they located the young jack hare hopping around on his own, and it occurred to them that with all his friends taken prisoner he was probably leading a rather lonely life.

'Well?' he asked rather nervously. 'What did your wise one say?'

Young Black Tip lay down so that he was almost speaking into one of the hare's long ears. 'He said that if your friends use their wits when they're being chased in the open field, there are ways they can out-run the gazehounds.'

The hare twitched his ears, and keeping one eye on Scab and the other on Young Black Tip, asked, 'What are these ways?'

'They can lead the gazehounds into the blinding light of day,' said Scab.

'Make them stumble on patches of water,' said Young Black Tip.

'Head for the first gap they see.'

'And keep going. He says the gazehounds tire quickly.'

'Your friend is very wise,' replied the hare. 'I suppose we do waste too much time and energy running around the field. But then, you see, we are afraid of the unknown. It is only when we have to, that we make for the gap.'

'Well your friends better start making for it fast,' said Scab, 'or they won't make it at all.'

Still obviously uncomfortable in the presence of foxes, the hare hopped forward and nibbled nervously at the grass. It was difficult to know whether he thought his friends would be able to overcome their fear and accept the ideas, but at least he promised to tell them.

'Now,' said Young Black Tip, 'tell me about the other place. The place that's fenced in. If we went there, would we be in any danger from the gazehounds?'

The hare squinted at him with one eye. 'Not unless you go inside. Why?'

'Well, we just thought there might be some way to help the hares there too. Do you know any of them?'

The hare hopped forward again, and when he replied the cubs thought they detected a note of sadness in his voice. 'I know one,' he said. 'A doe.'

The cubs looked at each other, and Scab inquired, 'Is she a friend of yours?'

The hare nodded.

'Can you take us there?' asked Young Black Tip.

Again the hare nodded, and without another word set off across the hills. The cubs followed, and to their surprise found that not once did he hesitate or take a wrong turn. Perhaps, they concluded, it wasn't the first time he had gone to see the doe.

Eventually, they came to the outskirts of a town and the hare stopped. The cubs had often heard their parents tell of a visit they made to man's place, and they knew they must be careful. However, they needn't have worried. Man's place was just as alien to the hare, and he took them around it in a wide circle until they came to a small wood. There he showed them a field, just beyond the wood, that man had fenced in so that the gazehounds could chase the hares. From the cover of the wood, the cubs scanned the field with great curiosity. It lay beyond a small river and a line of tall willow trees. It was very wide and very long, and even to their sharp eyes appeared to be completely flat. However, the young hare explained that from one end to the other it rose gradually, and while the incline was hardly noticeable, it provided a gruelling course for both the hares and the gazehounds that had to run its length.

'What way is this chasing done?' asked Young Black Tip.

The hare hopped forward so as to show them what he was going to say. 'When man catches any hares, he puts them in a pen, up there at the top end of the field. The pen is separated from the rest of the field by a hedge. Then he makes them run down along a little path at the side — it's there under the willows — until they're at the lower end. There he lets them out one at a time so that the gazehounds can chase them back up the field. If they run fast enough they can escape back into the pen through holes in the bottom of the hedge.'

Even as the hare talked, the cubs noticed movement on the far side of the field, and sounds which suggested that man was arriving with his gazehounds. 'We better take cover,' he told them. 'It won't be long now.'

Following him into the trees, the cubs watched and

waited.   On the far side of the field they could see people gathering in great numbers.   They seemed to be walking aimlessly around, and some had gazehounds on a leash.

'What are they doing?' asked Scab.

The young hare was sitting upright, his long ears twitching to every sound.   'They're waiting for the hares to go down the path so that the chase can begin.'

Suddenly there was a lot of shouting and the cubs ventured forwards, necks strained upwards, to try and find out what was happening.   On the far side of the field they could now see row upon row of people, standing in an open building, waving and cheering.   And a quiver of excitement ran through the cubs as they spotted two gazehounds streaking up the middle of the field in pursuit of a hare.   The hare was running for all it was worth, but the hounds closed in on it with great rapidity.   It twisted and turned, but to no avail.   There was an anguished scream, and the hounds began to pull it apart.   A red-coated horseman galloped past, while men ran to take the remains of the hare from the hounds and put them back on leashes.

The young hare lowered his head and began to shiver. Seeing that the fear was beginning to grip him again, Young Black Tip said, 'You told us the gazehounds can't get out. Isn't that right?'

The hare nodded, and the thought seemed to have a calming effect on him.

'Good,' said Young Black Tip, 'We want to get closer.'

'You can only go as far as the river,' the hare told him. 'Over there, under the willows.'

'Will you come with us and show us?' asked Scab.

Somewhat reluctantly, the hare agreed.   Leaving the wood they crept down into a meadow and over to the bank of the river.   It was a slow-moving river, overgrown with reeds and long grass.   The willows were on the far bank, and the cubs could hear long-tailed tits chirping in the branches, apparently unaware of the life and death struggle that was taking place in the field beneath them.

'The river helps to keep the hares in on this side of the field,' the hare explained.   'The rest of the field has high fences around it.'

Across from them, on the far bank, the cubs could see the

narrow path running down the riverbank. It was between two low netting-wire fences, and now they could also see hares hopping rather hesitantly along it.

'Where does the path take them?' asked Young Black Tip.

'We call it death row,' said the hare. 'They are driven down the path into a long, low house. There they wait their turn.'

'You mean, to run?' asked Scab.

The hare nodded. 'When the shutter goes up, they know their time has come to run from the gazehounds. If they can make it back up to the end of the field they can escape back into the pen. If they can't, it's death.'

'You must hate man as much as we do,' remarked Young Black Tip.

There was another cheer from the far side of the field, and the hare said, 'We hate what he does to us.'

The red-coated horseman who had galloped up the field after two more gazehounds, took out a coloured handkerchief and waved it to indicate which one was considered to have scored the most points.

'What about your doe?' continued Young Black Tip. 'Have you seen her?'

The hare shivered and shook his head. 'She might be still up in the pen — if she hasn't already been driven down to death row.'

'What are we waiting for?' asked Scab. 'Let's find out.'

Hoping they wouldn't be seen, they took off up along the river until they came to the pen where the hares were kept. There, man had laid a wooden plank across as a makeshift footbridge, and the cubs waited while the hare crossed over and hopped up close to the fence.

If the cubs were afraid that their presence might frighten the hares, there was no need to be. The hares were too numbed with fear of the gazehounds to feel any fear of foxes. Nor did they pay much attention to the young jack hare as he nosed his way nervously along the fence.

Scab was about to remark on this when suddenly the young hare sat up. His shivers had gone, and they could see he had located the doe on the other side.

'Ask her why they can't jump the low fence on the path and cross the river,' urged Young Black Tip.

The doe whispered something, and the young jack hare told him, 'They can't get a good enough run at it.   Anyway, they're afraid they might land in the river and drown.'

'If we can find a way to cross it, will they come?' asked Young Black Tip.

The young hare consulted the doe again.   'She's not sure.' Perhaps if they can get someone to lead the way.'

'What about her?   Will she do it?'

The cubs watched as the two of them whispered to each other through the wire once more.   Then the jack hare told them, 'She says she's willing to give it a try, provided I show her what to do.'   He began to shiver again, adding, 'And provided she hasn't gone to death row.'

'Right,' said Young Black Tip, 'tell her we'll be back as soon as we can figure out what to do.'

For the remainder of the day, the cubs and the hare lay in the wood, waiting for darkness and trying to figure out how they could help the other hares escape from the gazehounds. They listened to the chirping of the long-tailed tits as they sported themselves in the willows.   They also listened to the shouts of man and, occasionally, the screams of hares as the gazehounds sported themselves in the field beyond the river.   They had no way of knowing how many hares succeeded in escaping back into the pen, but the young jack hare reckoned more would survive than if the chase were held out in the open fields.   Out in the open, and on strange ground, he explained, they wouldn't know where to go.   In the fenced field they had been given practice runs, and at least they knew where they could return to the pen if they could run fast enough.

It all sounded a very strange and pointless exercise to the cubs, and whenever the hare would hop anxiously over to the edge of the wood, they wondered how they were going to get enough of his friends out and back to the hills so that they could hunt them for themselves.

Eventually man took his hounds and his dead hares and departed.   Night came.   The young jack hare went up to the pen to see if his doe was still alive, and the cubs returned to the river beneath the willows, to see how they were going to get the captive hares across.

The willows were strong and tall, and now as they looked at them, Black Tip noticed that one, which had grown out over the river towards the meadow, had been cut so that it would not offer a way of escape. However the stump still arched half-way across the water. 'They could easily jump across from that,' he said. Scab agreed. 'Of course they could. But how are you going to get hares to climb a tree?'

'All they have to do is hop up on to it and jump. And if the doe can do it, so can the others.'

At first the doe expressed grave doubts about the foxes' plan. What if man should see them, or, worse still, the gazehounds? Whatever about being caught in the open, they didn't want to be caught up a tree. Then, as she turned the idea over in her mind, the thought of a life in the hills with the young jack hare began to overcome her fears. Eventually, and with obvious foreboding, she agreed to give it a try. As for the others, she said she would ask them, but couldn't guarantee that they would agree to follow her.

Morning came, and man returned with his gazehounds, his flags, his shouts and his cheers. Up in the pen the doe waited to be driven down to death row. Across in the woods the young jack hare waited with the foxes and wondered if their plan would work. One by one the captive hares kept hopping down the path. One by one they continued to pass the arched tree stump, and whatever about the young hare, it wasn't long before the cubs began to despair. Indeed, they were beginning to wonder if something had gone wrong, when Scab said, 'There she is. She's at the tree!'

They held their breath, and the young hare began to shiver. 'She'll never do it,' he whimpered.

The doe had stopped at the arched stump, and they could see she was glancing in the direction of man and his gaze-hounds, as if she was wondering what she should do.

'Go on,' urged Scab to himself. 'Up you go.'

Still the doe hestitated. Other hares had stopped back along the path, waiting to see what she was going to do. She turned her head and looked up at the tree stump. Then, with almost effortless ease, she jumped up on to it and hopped out to the end. There, however, she hesitated again.

'Why is she waiting?' asked Young Black Tip.

'Because it is not in our nature to do things like that,' said the young hare.

'Jump,' whispered Young Black Tip. He could see that the other hares were still stopped on the path, wondering what to do. 'Jump,' he repeated, willing her on silently.

Scab turned to the young hare. 'Maybe it's you she's waiting for. She said she would do it if you showed her.'

The young hare immediately raced over to the river bank, and seeing him, the doe sat up. He hopped around, and whatever words of encouragement he spoke, the cubs saw the doe bracing herself. Then she gave a mighty leap, sailed clear across the river and landed safely on the bank. Turning around, she looked up at the stump, expecting the others to follow. There was no sign of them, and she hopped forward, waiting for them to make a move.

Seeing that the other hares were still hesitating, and that the moment of decision was slipping past, Young Black Tip ran over to the river, swam across and jumped up over the low fence on to the path. Immediately the hares began to move down towards the tree stump. There they stopped, like a herd of sheep, uncertain what to do. Young Black Tip lay down so as not to make them panic.

The hares were looking up at the tree stump now, just as the doe had done. Suddenly there was a cheer from the people on the far side of the field, and the thud of pads as the gazehounds raced past. The hares turned and listened. They were nervous, undecided. Yet even as he watched them, Young Black Tip knew in his heart what they were going to do. And when, a moment later, they hopped on down the path, he wasn't surprised. It was the fear of the fear Old Sage Brush had spoken of. The hares had chosen to meet the gazehounds in the field they knew, rather than risk meeting them in a field they didn't know. They had chosen death row instead of freedom.

Disgusted and disappointed, Young Black Tip raced down the path, scattering any hares that remained. Without stopping, he ran up the arched tree stump and leapt across the river. Scab was waiting for him, but the young jack hare and the doe had gone.

Both cubs were certain that when they returned to the birches they would receive a strong reprimand from Old

Sage Brush, or at the very least, some indication of his disapproval.   They should have known, however, that this was not the old fox's way.   The other cubs giggled, of course, but he listened in silence as they told how they had only succeeded in releasing one hare, and it had got away.

'You were right,' admitted Young Black Tip.   'They've a blind spot between their ears as well as their eyes.   I mean, how can you help them if they won't help themselves?'

'All they had to do was jump,' Scab recalled.   'Then we'd have had all the hares we needed.'

'It was just too big a jump for them to make,' said Old Sage Brush.   'It was like asking them to act like squirrels instead of hares, climb instead of run.   You see, running is the only defence they know.   They were given speed instead of brains.'

'So were some cubs I could mention,' chided Little Running Fox.   'I think it was stupid to try and get a hare to climb a tree.'

'Well one did,' retorted her brother.

'One,' said Little Running Fox, 'and she wasn't long in showing you a clean pair of heels!'

Twinkle sniggered.   'The jack hare didn't hang around to say thanks either.'

'What do you expect?' said Scab.

'Anyway,' added Little Running Fox, 'it serves you right, both of you, thinking you knew better than your elders.'

'Well, at least we tried,' said Scab.   'And it could have worked.'

'Sometimes,' the old fox suggested, 'it is just as important to know when you cannot win, as it is to know when you can.'   The two cubs had lowered their heads, and sensing that they were feeling rather crestfallen, he added, 'But then again, you might look at it another way.'

Young Black Tip raised his head: 'What way's that?'

'Well,' said Old Sage Brush, 'when you think of it, there are two hares out there now, and when it comes to putting hares back on the hills, all it needs is two. . .'

The other cubs looked at each other.   Suddenly they weren't so sure they had won the argument, or who had won the battle of the gazehounds — Young Black Tip and Scab, or the two hares.

14: A Time of War

THE BERRIES ON THE spindle trees had turned from green to pink and soon they would become what Young Black Tip had called the colour of blood. The haws were already an inconspicuous red, while the sloes had ripened to a rich frosty black. Only the ivy, it seemed, had still to develop its seed. Nature had arranged things so that the ivy flowered late, thus providing insects with a final source of sustenance before the winter came.

Already the days had turned cold, and the swallows had left in search of sunnier places. The small birds that remained scrambled among the branches to feed while the berries lasted. If they were lucky, enough would be left to see them through the winter. If not, some of them would die.

For the moment, however, the hedgerows were teeming with life, and the valley which the foxes knew as the Land of Sinna was aflame with colour. In the evening, the sun was a ball of fire in a crimson sky, and in the morning it rose to reveal a countryside whose leaves were turning the most beautiful shades of brown, red and gold.

In the fullness of time, the coats of the cubs had also changed colour. Like the leaves on the trees, they varied, but in general they had become a richer brown. It was a subtle change, as subtle as the change in the season itself, but it was something that didn't escape the notice of the trapper. However, even now as they groomed each other under a hawthorn hedge, the cubs themselves were completely unaware of it.

Old Sage Brush was dozing beneath broad leaves of burdock. The cubs were sitting nearby, and even though the old fox didn't appear to be listening, he had one ear cocked and knew their thoughts were not on their fur, but on more distant things . . .

'Did you ever wonder?' said Twinkle.

Little Running Fox, who was running her teeth through the fur on Twinkle's head, stopped and asked, 'Wonder what?'

'What lies beyond the hills.'

'Sometimes I do.'

'So do I,' said Young Black Tip. 'And some night soon I'm going to find out.'

Scat edged closer. 'Me too. Who knows what we'll find?'

'Maybe you'll just find more trouble,' said Twinkle.

Young Black Tip ignored her. 'I think there are whole new areas over there, just waiting for us to move in.'

'Places with plenty of food,' added Scat. 'And plenty of vixens.'

Twinkle snorted and remarked, 'You'll be lucky.'

The dogs continued to ignore her, and Young Black Tip went on, 'There are probably so many hares over there we won't know what to do with them. And rabbits too, not like the ones we have here. No sleepy sickness or anything.'

'Maybe there's even a place where man hasn't been to,' said Scat. 'A place like the glen where everything can be as it should be. What do you think Scab?'

Scab had been silent. His fur, or what was left of it, didn't need much grooming. 'I don't know,' he said. 'I haven't made up my mind yet what I'm going to do.'

'You mean you're not sure if you're going to go?' asked Scat.

'I told you, I haven't made my mind up. I mean, who's to say there's not another big dog with a stumpy tail waiting over there to chase us. Or more gazehounds, or howling dogs. At least here we know where to run.'

'But how are you going to find out if you don't go?' asked Young Black Tip.

Above them, a flock of finches had begun to flit through

the branches as they fed on haws and elderberries, and before Scab could answer, there was a pattering like the sound of falling hailstones.   Startled, the cubs jumped up and ran out into the field.   Only then did they realise that the noise had been caused by berries, shaken loose by the birds, falling on the broad leaves of burdock.   They laughed, and when the old fox got up and joined them, they made their way back to the bog.

'Sometimes,' said Old Sage Brush when they talked again about the birds.   'Sometimes I wish I could see them.'

Strange as it may seem, it was the first time the cubs had ever heard the old fox regret the loss of his sight. Somehow he had always led them to believe that whatever the disadvantages, there was a lot to be gained from not being able to see.   Now they realised just how much man had taken from him.   If he could miss seeing the birds, how much must he miss seeing other things which were important to him?   And so they lay beneath the birches and talked to him about the birds and all the other things they had seen. Later, when they recalled once more the fright they had got from the falling berries, he chuckled in his usual contented old way, and they were glad.

'It may not have surprised you,' Twinkle told him, 'but it gave us an awful fright.'

The old fox nodded.   'So it would.'   He shifted slightly to make himself more comfortable and added, 'It may also have given nature the opportunity to play a little trick on you.'

'What trick?' asked Young Black Tip indignantly.

'Well, the plant with the large leaves also has very large prickly seeds, and unlike you they just can't take off whenever they are ready to go.'

'So?' asked Scat.

'So they hitch a ride.   You'll find one or two of them on your fur if I'm not mistaken.   That's the way the seeds disperse.'

Scab smiled, and as the others examined their fur, remarked, 'They'd have a job sticking to me!'

'But they have stuck to some of you,' continued Old Sage Brush, knowing by their silence that this was so.   'And it just serves to remind you.   Other things can play tricks as well as you, especially man.   It won't be long now until he comes after you with his choking hedge traps, his guns and his dogs.   So remember all that I've told you, and use it well.   Your life will depend on it.'

'And what about you?' asked Scab.   'What will you do?'

Old Sage Brush lifted his head towards the birch leaves which he now knew were beginning to fall, and said, 'I must remember them too.   Why do you think I've lived so long?'

Beyond the hills a half moon sat on its tail in the southern sky.   Thinly veiled by a wisp of grey cloud, it was watched over by a single star.   It was unusually big and bright, making the night an ideal one for hunting, and when the cubs had gone, Old Sage Brush also slipped away from the birches.

More and more the cubs were going their individual ways to hunt, and on a night when they could use their senses of sight and smell to full advantage, the old fox knew they wouldn't be back for some time.   He couldn't see the bright eye of gloomglow himself, of course, but they had told him how, even though it was only half open, it lit up the countryside.   As he made his way out of the bog, he could almost feel its soft light shining on his aged back, and he knew how lovely it must be beneath the trees at Beech Paw. Vickey was waiting for him there.   They touched noses in a gesture of affection, and lay down to talk.

'Well,' said Vickey, 'what do you think?   Are they ready?'

'As ready as they'll ever be.'

Vickey didn't say anything more for a moment, but the old fox could feel her relaxing.   He knew that his assurance was a great comfort to her, and his thoughts went back to the time she had asked him to show her and her friends the secret of survival.   That was before the last breeding season, when she was concerned that with so many foxes dying at the hands of man, they might all be wiped out.   It was the same concern that had prompted her to seek his help in rearing the cubs.

'I hope it hasn't been too much for you,' she said gently.

The old fox laughed.   'What else would keep me young?   Except perhaps a nice young vixen like yourself.'

Vickey nudged him and smiled.   'You'd better not let

Black Tip hear you saying that.'

Old Sage Brush chuckled with amusement and asked, 'Where is that mate of yours anyway?'

'Out hunting.   They all are.'

'All except us,' said a familiar voice.

'Ah, Sinnéad,' said the old fox. 'And She-la. Come, come, lie down here beside me.'

Sinnéad snuggled up beside her father and asked him, 'Well, what do you think?'

'What do I think about what?'

'The cubs, of course,'

'They're fine.   Why shouldn't they be?'

'You know what we mean,' said She-la.   'Are they ready?'

'Sure they'll soon be telling me what to do.'

The vixens laughed, and She-la said, 'I wouldn't be surprised.'

'Well then, what are you worrying about?'   They didn't reply, and he added, 'After all, they have discovered the difference between a rabbit and a sheep, haven't they?'

'We're serious,' said Sinnéad.

'So am I.'   The old fox gave her a fatherly nudge with his nose.   'They've found they can't catch a field mouse by the tail, but they can catch a fish with their own.   They know to stay clear of the stoat and be wary of the trapper.   They've learned how to see what they sense and sense what they see;   to tread a narrow path and walk in the water;   to hunt like the spider and run like the hare.   What more can you ask?'

'But what about the fun dogs?' asked Sinnéad.   'Do they know enough to deal with them?'

Old Sage Brush knew well what his daughter was thinking. It was the fun dogs that had cost him his sight and almost lost her her freedom.   So he said, 'Didn't they confuse the fun dogs and free the badger?'

'But what about Scab?' inquired She-la.

'What about him?   Didn't he nearly drive the big dog mad, and get away from the mites that were driving himself mad?'

'But what about the gazehounds?' asked Vickey.

'And the howling dogs?' added Sinnéad.

'They faced up to the gazehounds didn't they?   Snatched

a hare from under their very noses.   It may not seem much, but it took a lot of courage to do that.   It also means you'll have hares on the hills again come your next breeding season.'

'But what about the howling dogs?' repeated Sinnéad.

'Don't worry.   They'll deal with them when the time comes, just as we dealt with them when they were after you.' The old fox raised his nose to savour the scents of the night.   'Now, tell me about your new vixen.   How is she?'

'She's staying with me, up in the blackthorns,' She-la informed him.

'She's still very shocked,' added Vickey.   'I don't know when she'll venture out again.'

'Give her time,' said the old fox.   'Time heals all things, even death.   When the breeding season comes around again, who knows, perhaps she will find another mate and the comfort of a new family.'

The half moon had now moved away across the hills from the star that had shone above it.   The vixens thanked Old Sage Brush for what he had done for their cubs, and he left to return to the bog.

A late autumn storm lashed the Land of Sinna.   It blew throughout the night, driving rain across the valley and bending the trees until they almost broke.   Over in the bog, the cubs lay and listened as the wind whipped the willowy branches of the birches to a frenzy.   Although they wouldn't admit it to Old Sage Brush or even to each other, they were full of foreboding.   In their mind's eye they could see the shadowy figures of horsemen galloping across the hills, and hear the eerie howling of the dogs in the wind.   It was no night for hunting, and they were glad. Somehow the fields beyond the bog, which had become so familiar to them, seemed terribly dark and full of danger. Everything would be sitting tight, just like themselves, waiting for the storm to pass, so they snuggled in close to the old fox, and drifted into an uneasy sleep.

By morning, the storm had blown itself out.   The sky was bright and it was very cold.   Overnight, it seemed, the leaves had gone and the countryside was bare.   The elder bushes had been stripped to the bone, the hardy haws

thinned out. Now the thrushes clung to the swaying
branches of the rowan tree to feed on its few remaining
fruits. Only the berries of the spindle tree stood out, a
striking splash of crimson above the blackthorns.

All this the cubs took in as they made their way through
the fields. Having fasted during the night, they were
hungry, and were hoping that they might find a pheasant or
two that had been blown off course. They were midway
between the bog and Beech Paw when a strange noise came
to their ears. However, it wasn't the crow of a cock
pheasant or the flap of wings which they might have hoped
for.

They stopped and Twinkle whispered, 'What is it?'

None of them answered. They were listening, trying to
make out what it was. A sort of drumming noise, shouts
. . . a bark?

Suddenly a pack of brown and white hounds came spilling
out into the field, and no sooner did the cubs realise that the
howling dogs were almost upon them, than they looked up
to see red-coated horsemen thundering down across the
hedge as if they were dropping from the sky.

Like an exploding star, the cubs turned and scattered in all
directions. Behind them came the chilling chorus of the
howling dogs and the call of the hunting horn. The dogs
they dreaded above all others were after them. Their
nightmare had come true. The hunt was on.

After the first few panic-stricken moments, they tried to
compose themselves. Old Sage Brush had warned them;
they mustn't give in to the fear of the fear. They were
leaving a strong scent, too strong for comfort, so they
decided to split up. Scab and the two vixens headed for
the bog, while Scat and Young Black Tip made for Beech
Paw. Both places, they felt should provide them with the
refuge they needed.

The hounds were confused. But not for long. They cast
about, uncertain which way to go. Then they were off
again in full cry, and soon it became obvious that their
quarry was Young Black Tip and Scat.

The two cubs were making for Beech Paw as fast as they
could, but before they reached it, they almost collided with
Black Tip and Skulking Dog.

'The howling dogs,' gasped Young Black Tip. 'They're after us.'

'We thought as much,' said his father. 'We were on our way to warn you.'

'We went out hunting when the storm eased,' Skulking Dog explained, 'and when we went back our earths were blocked.'

'All of them?' asked Scat anxiously.

'Hop-along's safe,' Skulking Dog told him. 'And so's your mother. Man couldn't get into the blackthorns to block their earth, although he tried. Vickey and Sinnéad are up there with them. They're all safely underground.'

'Good,' gasped Young Black Tip. 'Still, we better keep the howling dogs away from them. And here they come.'

'Right, off you go,' said his father. 'We'll try and draw them off.'

The howling dogs, however, were not be deflected. For some reason, they had chosen to follow the scent of Young Black Tip and Scat, and they continued to do so.

Having decided to stay clear of Beech Paw, the cubs changed course. With tails flailing, they flung themselves down the side of the valley towards the river where it left the dam. Old Sage Brush had told them the day they had learned to swim, that if they were ever pursued by the howling dogs, they should make for the river, and that was what they now proceeded to do.

To their relief they found that Ratwiddle had gone from his usual haunt among the alder trees and it occurred to them that while he might be a bit scatter-brained, he knew when to make himself scarce! Jumping into the river, they swam with the current for some distance before climbing out on to the far bank. The wind had almost died away now, but what was left was blowing downstream. With a little luck their scent would be carried far enough down the river to give them a breathing space.

Beyond the meadows, they cut across a farm where many cows were grazing. The howling dogs had now crossed the river, and the horsemen weren't far behind. Perhaps, they thought, if they mixed with the cattle, it would absorb their scent and maybe even throw the howling dogs off their trail. It was a good idea, but it was not to be. Old Sage

Brush had not exaggerated when he told them the noses of the howling dogs were second to none. Shortly after they left the farm, a renewed outburst of howling told them the hounds had disentangled the scents and were coming after them again. Heading down with the wind as they had been taught to do, they doubled back across the river. On the far side they took cover in a clump of weeds and lay down to get their breath back.

'It's not going to be easy to shake them off,' panted Scat.

'I didn't think it would be,' said Young Black Tip. 'Come on, let's head for that patch of evergreens up on the hill. Perhaps we can lose them in there.'

Whatever about the smell of cattle, the smell of pine trees was something else. Young Black Tip had been born on the very edge of a plantation; Scat not much farther away. And even though, thanks to Scab, that plantation had been burned down, they would always remember the strong sweet smell that emanated from it.

It was only when they reached the evergreens, that they realised they were the same ones from which Vickey and Black Tip had watched them the day they had almost been drowned by the flood. Panting from the exertion of the climb, they lay down just inside the trees and watched their pursuers gathering at the river. The howling dogs were running in through the shallows, sniffing the air as they tried to pick up the scent again. The red-coated horsemen had caught up with them, but some of the other riders had fallen behind and were strung out across the meadows.

'Here they come,' said Scat.

Seeing the howling dogs crossing the river, Young Black Tip glanced up towards the dam, saying, 'I wish the flood would come and wash them away.'

Scat smiled. 'No such luck.'

They looked at each other and Scat said, 'Well, this is where we part company.'

Young Black Tip nodded. 'Which way do you want to go?'

Any way. It's all the same to me.'

'Didn't your parents tell you that you should always run with the wind? Off you go. I'll head back up the valley and see where I can go from there.'

'I hope you find a land full of hares,' said Scat.

Young Black Tip smiled, 'And I hope you find a land full of vixens!'

They wished each other luck, and parted.   For a moment Young Black Tip paused to watch as his little friend scurried away through the trees.   At the same time, the sound of the howling dogs came to his ears.   Not knowing if the dogs would find their scent, or if they did, which one of them they would follow, he took off in the opposite direction as fast as he could.

As it turned out, the howling dogs didn't spend much time in the evergreens.   Finding the smell of the pines too overpowering for their sensitive noses, they soon began to scour the surrounding fields.   Since Scat had taken off with the wind, Young Black Tip was running into it, and it was inevitable that it was his scent they should find.   Having skirted around the bottom of Beech Paw, he was just beyond the line of trees when he heard their familiar cry.   Looking back, he saw them streaming down the fields towards him, and knew immediately it was his scent they had found. The evergreens had not brought an end to the hunt as he had hoped;   they had only given him another head start.

Taking off once more, he made a bee-line for the meadows. The soft ground, he had noticed, didn't suit the horse, and he hoped it would make the going harder for the howling dogs too.   He also wanted to keep them well away from Beech Paw and the bog.   At the back of his mind he could still hear Old Sage Brush telling him to use the river, and so he proceeded to cross and recross it in an effort to break his trail of scent.

As the day wore on, however, Young Black Tip discovered that it wasn't only a strong sense of smell that the howling dogs possessed.   They were also strong-willed, and had the stamina to keep going regardless of any delays or diversions he could contrive to put in their way.   Gradually he began to tire, and slowly but surely the dogs began to close the gap.

Although Young Black Tip had kept on the move, he had circled and doubled back numerous times to try and confuse his pursuers, and thus had managed to remain in the same general area, the area he knew best.   He reckoned Old Sage

Brush and the other cubs would be aware of what was happening. So would the foxes up at Beech Paw, including his parents. At the same time he realised there was nothing any of them could do to help him. Nor could he put them at risk by trying to join them. He had no choice but to keep going.

Finding himself not far from the glen, he thought of the lovely time they had spent there the day of the badger dig. He had heard that after the mayhem the trapper's big dog had caused, when it had almost caught Scab, the people in the glen had closed the hole in the fence. There were probably other ways to get in, but he feared that by the time he found them, the howling dogs would be on him.

Looking around, he could see there was very little other cover, as many of the hedges had been removed to make bigger fields for growing grain. This was a problem that had also confronted Scab, but at least the crops had given Scab the cover he needed. Now the fields were bare.

As Young Black Tip weighed all these things up, he saw that the farmers had already sown some of their winter barley and wheat, and several fields were bearded with new growth, like a sparse covering of grass. The soil beneath was still soft, and hoping that the going might be too heavy for the howling dogs, he set off up across them.

As it so happened, the hounds were now heading into a cultivated area that their masters wished to avoid. However, there was no stopping them. They were closing in for the kill, and so, as the horsemen galloped away to circle around the fields, the pack pressed on.

It was a gruelling climb, and by the time Young Black Tip reached the top of the fields, he found that whatever about the hounds the soft soil had sapped much of his own strength. When, a short time later, the horsemen rejoined the hounds and caught a glimpse of him, his sagging brush told them that he was now low in both body and spirit, and that the race was almost run.

Willing himself on, yet not knowing what to do, Young Black Tip kept going. He knew the howling dogs were closing in, and he wondered if he would end up like the cubs of the vixen who had sought refuge at Beech Paw. Or like the hares that were torn asunder by the gazehounds.

He recalled the agonising screams of the hares and wondered what the end would be like.   Suddenly he found himself at a river, but in his weariness couldn't tell what river it was.   For a moment he stood on the bank looking down at the water.   The day was almost spent, and a cold evening mist was swirling over the surface.   He knew he must take the plunge, but somehow he seemed to be trans-fixed, unable to move.   Then, as if in a dream, he became aware of his father standing beside him.

'Go on,' his father was saying gently.   'You can make it.'

Young Black Tip looked at him, unable now to distinguish between what was real and what was not.

His father smiled, and told him, 'You've done so well. Don't stop now.'

Not quite sure if he was imagining things, Young Black Tip nodded, and together they plunged into the river.   The water swallowed them up, and when, a second or so later the surface broke again only one of them emerged.   He looked around, swam to the far bank, and climbed out. Looking around again, he caught a glimpse of a sodden body floating down the river.   He also saw the howling dogs approaching the opposite bank.   His instinct was to try and help, but he knew that would only tell the dogs there was a fox in the water.   He had no option but to keep going. With a flick of his black-tipped tail, he turned and disappeared into the weeds.   As it happened, however, the dogs didn't see him.

On reaching the river, the pack began to mill around, sniffing, searching for the fox that had eluded them all day.   They could hear some of the riders galloping up behind them and then, farther back, they heard a fox barking.   Once again the cry of the hunting horn merged with the cry of the pack as both horsemen and hounds swept back towards Beech Paw.   They were not to know that the young dog fox they had been chasing was still in the river, and that they were now in pursuit of a vixen.

From their hiding place in the bog, Old Sage Brush and the other cubs had listened as the hunt had come and gone across the valley.   Then, as the day had drawn to a close, Little Running Fox, Twinkle and Scab had ventured out.   A white mist was settling over the bog, darkness was approaching and they reckoned the howling dogs must be fairly tired. If Young Black Tip was still alive, there was now a way to help him.

Having located the howling dogs at the river, and made her presence known to them from what she considered a safe distance, Little Running Fox headed back towards the bog. She hoped against hope that she wasn't too late. By this time the evening had become very cold and scents were beginning to weaken, but with Twinkle and Scab running alongside her, the howling dogs were well able to follow.

In the fields above the bog, the three of them stopped. Behind them they could hear the howling dogs and the few riders who had managed to keep up. Below lay the bog, hidden from view by the silvery mist. Waiting until the hounds were almost upon them, they split up, fanned out like the radial threads of a spider's web, and raced down towards the bog. Moments later, they disappeared into the mist. The howling dogs were close on their heels, and not realising what lay beneath the mist, charged in after them, followed by a few luckless riders.

The cubs, of course, could cross the bog with their eyes closed, thanks to Old Sage Brush, and now as they made their way back to the safety of the birches, they could hear horses, men and hounds floundering in the mire and the muddy pools that always lay in wait for the unsuspecting.

For what seemed an eternity, Old Sage Brush and the cubs lay beneath the birches and listened as man worked to extricate himself from the bog. They wondered what had happened to Young Black Tip, but couldn't risk going out until man had gone.

Darkness came, and man still struggled to retrieve the howling dogs. Back at the river, another creature also struggled to get a firmer footing. Young Black Tip had been washed on to the mud, and finding himself alive, staggered up on to the grassy bank. Realising that the howling dogs had gone at last, he sank down on to the soft grass to rest. Slowly but surely, the events of the day came flooding back into his mind. He remembered his father telling him to jump, and he wondered if he had been dreaming. Pushing himself up on to his feet, he began to search along the river bank, and not far away was pleased to find a faint scent which told him he had not been dreaming. His father *had* come to his aid.   So also, he suspected, had his sister, for he seemed to remember having heard her call.

From the direction of Beech Paw, Young Black Tip now heard the call of another vixen.   He knew immediately it was his mother, and he barked loudly in reply.   His first instinct was to return.   Then he looked up and saw the Great Running Fox taking off across the hills, and he knew it was time to go.   Turning his back to Beech Paw, he took off after it and disappeared into the night.

15: A Time of Peace

FROM A HIGH FIELD NEAR Beech Paw, Vickey heard Young Black Tip's answering call. All day she had waited and worried. She had no way of knowing if her mate had been able to help him. But now, at long last, she knew he was still alive. Old Sage Brush would also be happy to hear that call, she thought, and so would the other cubs. Then, even as she rejoiced, she felt a twinge of sadness, for somehow she sensed that Young Black Tip wasn't coming back.

'Run swift,' she whispered, and from the darkness beside her another voice added, 'Run free.' She looked around. It was the vixen who had lost her cubs to the howling dogs. At least, she thought, Young Black Tip was alive. And it was his right to go and find a territory of his own, just as it was Scat's right. It was also the right of Black Tip and Skulking Dog to go their own ways now. That's how it was with the dog foxes. Scab would stay, of course. Like Hop-along, Ratwiddle and Old Sage Brush, he would carry his scars better in the land he knew.

Little Running Fox and Twinkle would also stay — with Sinnéad, She-la and herself. That was their right. For it was the vixens who would hold the Land of Sinna. It was they who would keep it until the dogs returned. That might seem a long way off now, but it would soon come around. Then they could look forward to having new cubs. That would mark a new beginning, a time to love, and hope-fully, a time of peace.

Author's Note

In *Run Swift, Run Free*, as in my other books on the fox, I have endeavoured to keep the foxes and their environment as true to life as possible. At the same time it is a work of fiction and is not intended to stand up to scientific scrutiny. I have, for example, taken the liberty of assuming that foxes, like squirrels, can see in colour, although experts say they almost certainly see in black and white or shades of grey.

The Republic of Ireland, in common with Northern Ireland and Britain, is still rabies-free and continues to have a thriving export business in fox skins. In 1984–85, however, the figures showed an interesting change. About 58,000 skins were exported under licence, roughly the same as the previous season. But the number of wild skins was down about 10,000 to 28,000, and those farmed, up by about the same number to 30,000. Whether this will continue as a trend, remains to be seen.

In Northern Ireland, there have also been some welcome developments. Under the Wildlife Order 1985, those who trade in fox skins must now have a licence to do so. Furthermore, a number of methods of killing foxes have been banned, including the use of decoys such as sound recordings.

I would like to record my sincere thanks to the following: Fergal Mulloy and Tommy O'Shaughnessy, Forest and Wildlife Service, Dublin; Niall Sefton and Joe Furphy, Department of the Environment, Belfast; Aidan Brady, director, and staff, National Botanic Gardens, Dublin; Dr James O'Connor, entomologist, Natural History Museum, Dublin; Dr Derek Goodhue, senior lecturer in zoology, Trinity College, Dublin; Dr Neil Murray, sylviculturist, Dublin; Dr Jim Barry, zoologist, chairman, Cork SPCA and president, Munster Branch Irish Wildlife Federation; Tom O'Byrne, Monard Glen, Cork, chairman Cork Branch IWF; Dermot O'Driscoll, secretary and Ted O'Connor, inspector, Cork SPCA; Thaddeus Ryan, Master of Scarteen Hounds and committee member Irish Masters of Foxhounds Association; Ron Warrell, Dublin Regional Game Council farm, Bohernabreena, Co. Dublin; Paddy Jones, Bohernabreena; Pat and Jo Canavan, Borris Lodge, Co. Carlow; Larry and Kay Byrne, Bennekerry, Co. Carlow; John Hunt, Ballyfoyle, Co. Kilkenny; Dermot and Loretto McDonnell, and Johnny Hutton, Mortarstown, Carlow; Tom Birmingham, Ballytarsna, Co. Carlow; Joanne Gibbons, her daughters Sheila and Maureen and son Sean, the Quiet Man Coffee Shop, Cong, Co. Mayo; Chris and Jennie Crowley, Galway, their daughter Elizabeth and her husband Martin Byrnes, Oranmore; John Egan and Denis Mullins, Rathfarnham, Dublin; Dr Percy Patton, Terenure, Dublin; my neighbours Matt and Mary Maher; and my colleagues Jim Lynch and Michael Lally.

A special word of thanks to the late Tim Kelly, and his wife Kathleen, of Luggacurren, Co. Laois, for all the help they gave me; Colette Nolan, of Ashford, Co. Wicklow for sharing with me the knowledge she has gained from rearing her pet foxes; Cormac MacConnell for his excellent article on badger-baiting in *The Irish Press*; my neighbour John Fenner for his copy of *The Complete Book of the Greyhound*, compiled and edited by "The Rambler"; and my colleague, photographer Tom Holton of RTE.

For their continuing support and encouragement, my sincere thanks once again to my wife Fran, and daughters Michelle, Amanda, Samantha and Simone. Also a special thank you to my brother Bobby of the London City Mission, for the quotation from Ecclesiastes from which the chapter headings in this book are taken.

Tom McCaughren,
1986